THE RICHMOND THIEF

Lisa Boero

Copyright © 2016 Lisa Boero
All rights reserved.
ISBN: 099825990X
ISBN-13: 9780998259901
Library of Congress Control Number: 2016918417
Nerdy Girl Press, Marshfield, WI

Also by the author:
Murderers and Nerdy Girls Work Late
Bombers and Nerdy Girls Do Brunch
Kidnappers and Nerdy Girls Tie the Knot
"Kept afloat by a plucky heroine, like a yuppie version of Stephanie Plum."

—*Kirkus Reviews*

And *Hell Made Easy*, the first book in the Trilogy from Hell

For all of the Jane Austen fanatics in my family.

CHAPTER ONE

Too much cannot be written about the frailties of the fairer sex. Among the many recognized by all educated societies, I must add a note related to the scientific method. It has been my experience, reinforced by rigorous inquiry, that females do not have the robust mental processes required for the hard labors of scientific investigation.

—Lord Ephraim Randolph Booth, "Observations on the Scientific Method," *Philosophical Transactions of the Royal Society,* August 1809

Despite Lord Ephraim's learned observation, Althea leaned against the end of the old-fashioned settle, her head propped in her hand, reading the second volume of *The Natural History of British Insects.* Her sister-in-law, Jane, having succumbed to slumber after a very trying day, was gently dozing on the settle opposite her. This was how they usually spent their evenings in Dettamoor Park, and Lady Althea Trent did not see any reason why a freak spring snow, a broken carriage axle, and a forced refuge at a small shabby inn, incongruously named The Swan, should destroy their routine.

Althea shifted her position, rustling the folds of her black bombazine dress. It was still damp from her unfortunate fall into a snowbank, but that was what she deserved for leaping out of the carriage without waiting for assistance. She'd caught sight of a rare warbler on a tree branch above her. The bird did not wait for her to extricate herself from the snow but flew off in haste in the opposite direction. Fortunately, bombazine appeared to be designed for reckless widows. No amount of abuse ever seemed to affect its matte gloom.

Althea had been a widow for something over two years, but she hadn't yet thrown off the somber dresses. Black bombazine allowed her the freedom to conduct her daily observations, to tromp over the muddy fields of the park, to sit on the grassy slopes for specimen drawing, and even to wade into the lake for aquatic experiments with perfect equanimity. Lately, she had begun an examination of the mating behaviors of the speckled green frogs that lived contentedly among the bulrushes. She also continued to work most diligently on a treatise of the life cycle of the flesh-eating beetles that had consumed the last days of her dying husband. And probably her husband as well, now that she came to think of it.

It was Arthur's fondest wish to see the treatise published, but illness took him too soon. Instead, his notes lay bundled together, ready to be recopied into Althea's fine hand. If she were a man, she would be able to complete the work—or, better yet, improve upon her husband's solid but uninspiring theses—and submit it to the Royal Society. However, it seemed a hopeless business for a member of the weaker sex. Particularly when powerful members of the Royal Society, such as Lord Ephraim, seemed set against the very idea that women were as fit as men for scientific inquiry. And yet Althea couldn't put the idea entirely out of her mind. It gnawed at her until she knew that she must at least make the attempt. A fortuitous invitation from her husband's cousin to visit the family in London had provided the perfect opportunity to try her luck.

Besides, she could use a break from the seemingly endless number of men hanging around Somerset in search of a rich wife. How dear departed Arthur would have laughed to see her—the plain and studious Althea—a modern Penelope, beset on all sides by suitors. Unfortunately, no handsome Odysseus had yet appeared, so Althea had been forced to improvise all sorts of tricks to repel them.

The widow's weeds assisted her with this task. And she'd acquired a reputation for determined devotion to her lost spouse. A sigh and a pitiful look cast upward was usually enough to shame even the most ardent suitor. Although Squire Pettigrew, a ponderous young man whose sense of his importance went beyond what family prominence and ability should warrant, was without remedy.

Fortunately, dramatics and black bombazine would likely not be required in the drawing rooms of the great metropolis. Although Althea had heard tales of the lengths to which some fortune-hunting men would go to secure a prosperous bride, she wasn't beautiful or titled enough to tempt the fashionable men of Cousin Bella's set. And she was sure that her cousins would prevent her from falling prey to the more unscrupulous characters. As she understood it, Bella had three sons: two on the town, the Earl of Bingham and Lord Charles Carlton, and one fighting in Spain, Colonel Augustus Carlton, who might return at any moment to the delights of society. Althea reasoned that with two, or perhaps three, such escorts, she might pass her time in London unmolested and free to pursue her quest for publication with the Royal Society.

And dear Jane would always lend assistance. She was the ostensible reason Althea had thrown off her comforts to venture forth on a London expedition to the house of Arthur's cousins. Jane fondly remembered her own years upon the town, before her brother's ill health and scientific eccentricities had forced her into country retirement. Cousin Bella's fortuitous marriage and present exalted position would ensure that Althea and Jane met only the best people—the noble and envied members of the ton. Bella could be counted on to live in a whirl of social activity, and it would be lovely to see Jane in the middle of it all, happy again.

Althea closed the book, stood up, and shook out the folds of her skirt. She lifted a still-damp boot to the warmth of the fire. Then, leaning her slight frame against the mantel, she stared into the flames, wondering what Arthur would make of their journey. Although theirs was no love match, she had come to respect Arthur as a man as much as she'd always respected his alarming intellect. His judgment had been unerring, even in the unusual selection of the daughter of his physician to be the second Lady Trent.

Althea longed for her husband's steady guidance more than ever. And she did not just have herself to guide. Young Arthur, showing signs of precocious intelligence, had been sent to study with Mr. Pellham. Althea already missed him terribly. Perhaps when this London adventure was over, Mr.

Pellham would spare him to visit Althea for a month's vacation at Dettamoor Park. How lovely that would be!

The door to the coffee room opened suddenly, and Althea jumped back.

"I beg your pardon, madam," the stranger said, startled himself. He was a tall man, something beyond middle age, but still powerfully built. He was dressed in the manner of a country gentleman, with high boots, buckskin breeches, and a loose-fitting coat, with a rumpled drab greatcoat thrown over his shoulders. Powdery snow clung to his hair and clothes.

Although Althea was naturally wary of men who arrived at shabby inns at night, she tried to disguise her fear. "No matter, sir. You've just caught me in a moment of reverie. Do come warm yourself by the fire. You must be fearfully cold after venturing forth on a night like this." She grabbed the iron poker, just in case she would have to use it, and moved to stand by the settle where Jane continued her uninterrupted slumber.

"I thank you kindly, madam. 'Tis a wicked night to be sure." He removed his greatcoat, threw it over a chair pulled up to the round table on the other side of the room, and advanced to the fireplace.

Althea walked back to the fire and made a show of sticking the poker in the flames. If he came near her, he would get a red-hot poker in the face.

However, the man did not seem to be troubled by her actions. Instead, he gave her a short bow. "James Read, at your service."

Upon closer inspection, Althea could see a certain level of disorder in Mr. Read's dress. His waistcoat was without a bottom button, and his breeches were not entirely free from mottled stains at the knees. He pulled on the cravat at his throat, loosening its wrinkled folds, and Althea pushed the poker farther into the fire.

She bobbed her head in reply. "Lady Trent. And this is my dear sister, Miss Trent, who, as you can see, is quite the worse for wear this evening."

She studied Mr. Read another moment. Although disordered, his coat was clearly cut by an expert tailor. Such a tailor was not likely to be seen outside of London. This implied that he too was an unusual visitor for an establishment such as The Swan. Besides, the name struck her as familiar.

Her shoulders relaxed. "Are you not Magistrate Read of Bow Street fame?"

"I am magistrate of Bow Street. May I infer that your ladyship is a reader of the London periodicals?"

Althea met his gaze squarely with her large brown eyes. "Only the most sensational ones, I assure you. My home is in Somerset, so we receive the *Hue and Cry* when it is rumpled and out of date to the rest of the world." She left the poker and sat down, leaning back against the smooth wood of the settle. "Nonetheless, the exploits of Bow Street occupied many a fine evening. My late husband was particularly interested in the scientific aspects of criminal detection."

Mr. Read sat down upon the opposite seat. He picked up Althea's book, a frown between his brows. "I see you have been occupied with more than just the periodicals." He handed her the book.

"Oh yes, I find the natural world fascinating. One can learn so much about the human condition by studying plants and animals."

"And insects?"

Althea tried to repress a smile. "Most definitely. Take, for example, the bees. The queen manages the whole enterprise without once leaving her cozy throne. That is a metaphor for any number of women of my acquaintance."

"Is it indeed? But your ladyship is an unusual woman to draw the connection."

"We are not all of us flighty insubstantial beings, Mr. Read. My husband was a Fellow of the Royal Society, and although his health did not permit him to travel much, he was able to prepare quite a number of valuable monographs. I naturally assisted him with these efforts. Perhaps you have chanced to read *A Comprehensive Study of the Beetles of Somerset* or *An Examination of the Toads of England*?" Mr. Read shook his head, an amused smile playing about his grizzled mouth. "No? Well, they were both very fine in their way and quite worth the effort. I drew the illustrations, so perhaps I am not a fair judge, but several of the Society members were quite effusive in their praise."

"I'm sure the monographs are above reproach. Unfortunately, I am not a man of science and so may not be able to appreciate their worth."

Althea frowned. "I can see I am prattling on quite abominably when you are probably wishing to enjoy the warmth of the fire in peace."

"No, Lady Trent, nothing can be farther from the truth. I asked our good host before I came in here to bring me a hot rum punch and would like nothing better than to continue this conversation over a glass. Or perhaps a lighter beverage? A ratafia? Or wine? Although I can't vouch for it being above vinegar in a place like this."

Althea wrinkled her nose. "We met with a series of vexing delays on our way to London, else we should not have stopped here. I gave Mrs. Nelson strict instructions about the airing of sheets, so I shall keep hope alive until the bitter end."

Mr. Read smiled. "Then perhaps the punch would be safest."

As if on cue, Mr. Nelson appeared with a bowl of steaming liquid. "Ah, Lady Trent," he said in surprise. "I had thought you retired for the evening."

Althea held up the book. "I have been unaccountably detained, but please let your kind mistress know that Miss Trent and I shall retire shortly."

Mr. Nelson set the bowl on the table, all affability and obsequiousness. "Very good, Lady Trent. Shall I fetch another glass?"

Mr. Read looked at Althea for confirmation. She nodded.

"I won't be but a moment now," Mr. Nelson said earnestly, and he scurried out of the room.

Mr. Read went to the table, and Althea followed. He moved the ladle around and around the liquid, seemingly lost in thought.

Althea watched his profile for a moment and then said, "I think you must be working on some very difficult crime at the moment. Perhaps something in this vicinity, which takes you to undesirable inns? Whenever I have to wrestle with knotty issues, I always find that speaking aloud helps the mind fit the pieces into place."

Mr. Read looked up, surprised.

Althea arched her brows, but said nothing.

"Your ladyship is too quick by half. Here, madam." He ladled a cup of the steaming brew into the glass and handed it to her.

Mr. Nelson appeared with another glass on a tray and then disappeared just as quickly, walking backward out the door, doubled over in a bow.

"That fellow will do himself a mischief walking like that." Mr. Read poured a glass of rum punch and held it aloft. "To your ladyship's health."

"Very pretty, sir." She took a sip. To her great surprise, the punch was extremely well blended, sweet, and intoxicating.

Mr. Read pulled out a chair and gestured for her to be seated at the table. She complied and then settled her black skirts and sipped her punch.

He took the seat opposite her. "Indeed, madam, you are correct. I have been deep in thought."

"Given your dress, you have also been enjoying the delights of a country house," she said.

He nodded. "I ought to be closer to London by now, but I got a late start this afternoon, and the weather overset all my plans."

"And those plans are? Or perhaps you do not care to confide in a stranger?"

"We had word that the Richmond Thief was to strike again at Lord Woolwich's estate not ten miles from here. But either it was a false report or word of our intention must have leaked. There was no robbery."

"The Richmond Thief?"

"If you have heard of Bow Street, you must also have heard of him. He is the most cunning, most devious jewel thief of our times."

"Despite my perusal of the *Hue and Cry*, I'm afraid the exploits of the Richmond Thief are quite unknown to me."

"Then perhaps I should not enlighten your ladyship. I would not want to worry you unnecessarily."

"No, sir, please do. I have never had the beauty to wear much jewelry, so I have no fear of thieves, even very clever ones."

Mr. Read smiled, causing deep wrinkles to form all the way up his cheeks. "The Richmond Thief steals into houses and comes out again without leaving a trace of his presence. The jewels are simply gone."

"They cannot be traced? Although the settings may be changed, fine gems must always be recognizable."

"We think he carries them abroad for sale."

"Ah. Very difficult in these uncertain times, but then Mr. Bonaparte has an exquisite court to maintain." She paused, considering the matter. "If the thief leaves no trace, then how can you be certain that it is the Richmond Thief? Perhaps there are several thieves working in tandem."

"It has been my experience that where there is more than one, they eventually come to blows. The Richmond Thief has successfully eluded capture these two years or more. It is the care with which he steals that marks his crimes. He is so very neat that there is no sign of entry, and nothing but jewelry is ever taken."

"A puzzle indeed. Why is he called the Richmond Thief?"

"Her Grace, the Duchess of Richmond, was the first victim. A fine pair of ruby earrings, just purchased from the jeweler, went missing the night of a masked ball."

"Then she was a simpleton for leaving her jewelry box unlocked."

"Unlocked? No, no. The thief took the jeweler's box as well."

"So he does take something besides the jewels."

Mr. Read nodded ruefully. "I stand corrected."

At that moment, Jane stirred and opened her eyes. She looked at the pair sitting cozily over the bowl of punch. Her eyes narrowed. "Althea, dear?"

Althea recognized the beginning of a scold. "Yes, Jane, I know we should retire. I sent Sally up to prepare for us. Magistrate Read, may I present my sister, Miss Trent?"

Jane struggled up stiffly out of the seat. She was a tall woman with a long straight nose and high cheekbones. Although still called handsome by her acquaintances, Jane's fine features were somewhat counteracted by a piercing look and a sharp tongue that she had not sought to curb once marooned at Dettamoor Park.

Mr. Read stood and bowed. "Enchanted, Miss Trent. Would you care to join us in a glass of rum punch?"

Jane curtsied ever so slightly. "No, thank you, sir." She looked pointedly at Althea. "It is quite late."

Althea finished her punch with a quick and not altogether ladylike gulp. "Yes, I think we should retire." She held out a hand to Mr. Read, who took it briefly in his own. "Although we are not likely to meet again, it has been a great pleasure to make your acquaintance."

"Madam, believe me when I say that the pleasure is all mine."

"Humph," said Jane.

CHAPTER TWO

"I still say that it is unwise to talk to strangers at an inn, particularly an inn of that sort." Jane shuddered dramatically. "Why, I was kept awake all night listening to vermin gnaw away the walls."

They were finally on the road again, headed into London with thick rugs over their laps and hot bricks at their feet. The young maid, Sally, was fast asleep against the squabs, so Althea and Jane indulged in unfettered conversation. They flew through innumerable topics, but they always seemed to end up back at The Swan.

Althea laughed. "Surely you exaggerate. And I don't see that any harm came of a glass of punch. You should have tried it, by the way. It was very good."

"Probably brought in by smugglers. That Mr. Nelson had a shifty eye."

"Smugglers with good taste in rum. My dear, although I love you, let us make one thing clear. I am not on the hunt for a husband—or any kind of other dalliance, for that matter—so you can leave off warning me about every ineligible man who happens to cross my path. Besides, Magistrate Read was old enough to be my father."

"They're never too old for that sort of thing."

"My, my, this does smack of experience. Just what was the London season like in your day?"

"Same as it is now, I'm sure. Lots of pushy mamas trying to foist their simpering daughters off on the richest man who'll have them. A smattering of charming but inevitably penniless French émigrés. Rakes and ne'er-do-wells chasing after any woman with a guinea to her name. Men who should be settling down to the producing of an heir wasting their time on drink and cards and opera dancers."

"Sounds delightful."

Jane eyed her sternly. "It is. No trying to back out on me. You promised."

"I will suffer through anything just to keep you happy."

"It's not my happiness I care about. Look, child, although I never could understand why my brother thought that a girl barely out of the schoolroom would make a fit wife for a stodgy widower like him, he picked you. And you two seemed to get along just fine with your investigations and those tiresome papers about God knows what creepy-crawly thing. But now he's gone, and I will not have a lot of youth and beauty moldering away between the four walls of Dettamoor Park."

"I'll accept the compliment of beauty, although it is a gross exaggeration, but youth I cannot. A woman of seven and twenty is not a green girl."

"She is when she's never left Somerset."

Althea allowed Jane to feel that she had won the argument and moved on. She said, "Perhaps I shall finally accept Squire Pettigrew's most obliging offer of marriage. He is certainly persistent enough about it. There is no dissuading him."

"No woman of the least intelligence would ever consent to be his wife."

"If I was in straightened circumstances and not at all bookish, I'm sure I would find him unexceptionable. Besides, his mother was to blame for making him what he is. She taught him to think as he does on all matters."

"He would have done well to escape her clutches, but she had him under such firm control. Even now, her routines and habits are still fixed within his mind. He will never leave Somerset, mark my words."

Althea chuckled. "I hope you are right, dear Jane, because then I shall thoroughly enjoy my sojourn in London."

Althea pulled back the curtain from the window. For the last half an hour she could hear the sounds of coachmen and horses as the carriage swayed slowly over the cobblestone streets. The din of the great city was impressive to a country-bred woman.

"I apprehend from the increase of traffic and the foul smells that we are soon to reach Bella's house. Please direct me to what I am to see in Grosvenor Square," Althea said.

"Impudent girl," Jane replied. "The Marchioness of Levanwood lives in very different circumstances. Nothing to see in this part of town."

"Don't tell me we are passing by the gentlemen's clubs." Althea went as if to lean out and then felt a clawlike grip on her arm.

"Get back in here. Of course not. Do you think I'd let the coachman take you into St. James before your credit is even established in town?"

Althea sat back against the squabs. "I thought a rich widow didn't need credit." Jane frowned and Althea laughed. "Just teasing you, dear. The gentlemen may attend their clubs in peace, because I've no desire to join them in drinking and silly card games. The Royal Society is another matter, of course."

"A matter you will please leave off while we are in London. I know, although you have tried to hide it, that your heart is set on the publication of some sort of beetle monograph. But I beg you not to speak of it in company, for there is nothing so boring as a bookish woman."

"Speaking from experience again?"

Jane's eyes sparkled. "Mind your own business."

Cousin Bella lived in a large stone house in the most fashionable part of London, its gray facade adorned with Grecian cornices and columns. Althea and Jane were welcomed by a plump matron whose once notable beauty was now sadly faded and who was dressed for the afternoon in a heavy green gown that made her skin look sallow. On her head sat a large turban adorned with an elaborate ruby and gold brooch. The effect was startling and not altogether pleasant.

"My dear cousins! I had despaired of you! It is really too bad about this awful weather." Bella clasped Althea to her opulent bosom, nearly crushing Althea's ribs in the process. The smell of French perfume hung heavily in the air, causing Althea's nose to itch.

Bella repeated the procedure with Jane. "How I have looked forward to your visit. All the amusements, all of the parties. Why, Lady Shirling was just telling me about the masked ball she means to hold—how daring—and of course I have already spoken to Lady Jersey. For you must have vouchers as soon as possible. As you know, anyone who is anyone is seen at Almack's!"

Bella then grabbed Althea with one arm and Jane with the other and pushed them forward. "Come into the red salon. John and Charles are just wild to meet their cousin, and they haven't seen you in ages, Jane. And we've a lovely nuncheon set out—for you must be simply famished. I declare that there is nothing so fatiguing as a journey, is there not?"

Althea opened her mouth to reply, but Bella continued on. "Of course the marquess would be here to greet you as well except he had some business to attend to. Something with bankers and I know not what. Men can be so provoking!"

The doors to the red salon were held open by an upright footman in a smart blue livery, and the Marchioness of Levanwood bustled through them, dragging her visitors with her. "John, Charles, do bestir yourselves, I beg of you!"

Two young men looked up. One was standing by the marble chimney piece, nonchalantly twirling a quizzing glass on a long black silk cord. He was dressed in a coat of dark green wool cut tightly across his broad shoulders over a figured silk waistcoat that had a profusion of golden fobs at the watch pocket and a high starched cravat, which was looped in an intricate pattern around his neck. He wore skintight pantaloons on his shapely legs and black boots with a mirrorlike polish. He was decidedly handsome, with an aquiline nose, large dark eyes, and dark hair he allowed to curl around his face.

The younger one was rather less prepossessing. Charles sat in a chair with a large volume between his slim fingers. He set the book aside and rose as the ladies entered the room. He lacked his brother's height, and his figure was neat rather than attractive. He was dressed sensibly, without a dandy's affectations. His straight brown hair was cut short over his mild blue eyes. He was the first to reach Althea and Jane.

"Charles, dear, this is Lady Trent. Althea, my son, Charles," Bella said.

He grasped her hand and raised it briefly to his lips. "Lady Trent, how delighted I am to make your acquaintance. After so many years in the wilderness, we had quite given you up for lost."

Althea smiled. "Somerset is wild indeed, Lord Charles."

"If you would permit the impertinence, Charles will do just fine. We are family, after all."

"As you wish. And you may call me Althea if you like."

He smiled at her. "I do indeed."

"Come Charles, let John have a turn with our charming cousin." Bella pulled him away to speak to Jane.

The handsome young man came forward. "Delighted to meet my long-lost cousin and all that." He pecked at her hand and then let it fall. "Dare say but Mother won't have you paraded around town within a week—although society is still pretty thin."

"I'm sure, Lord Bingham," Althea replied, "that I will need guidance from all my dear family. I'm not used to moving in such elegant society."

"Devilish bore most of the time. Lots of tedious card parties and whatnot."

"I think your mother mentioned Almack's."

"Flat."

"I beg your pardon?"

"Dull, madam, deadly dull."

"Oh, how disheartening. Then what do you do for amusement, cousin?"

He opened his mouth to reply, but instead looked uncomfortable. "I'm sure you'll enjoy the balls just fine. That is, if you dance?"

"Perhaps. I mean, I have learned, if that's what you are asking. But no, I haven't decided if I should come out of mourning just yet."

"Black doesn't become you," he said.

Althea smiled at his abrupt manner. "I'm sure it doesn't. And I do have some colored gowns. But fashion is not really the point of mourning, is it?"

"Barbarous custom if you ask me, made up for the benefit of haberdashers and tailors and such. A refined society should not mandate a public display of emotion."

Bella jumped into the breach. "Now, John dear, Althea doesn't want to hear a lot of newfangled rubbish from those poet friends of yours. Please come and let us eat."

Althea was thrust into a chair by the fire and handed a glass of lemonade. A fine display of cold meats and pickles had been laid out on a low table. There were also delicate rolls and several types of cake. Althea perceived that Bella's idea of a nuncheon was quite expansive.

Bella eyed John suspiciously when he took a seat on the settee beside Althea. "Isn't this delightful," she said with a hint of anxiety in her voice.

Charles led Jane to another chair, and Bella hovered solicitously near the table. "Just like an alfresco picnic. I do so love a picnic. Charles, hand Miss Trent a glass of lemonade. So refreshing! There, dear, that's right. Oh, you both must try those little honey cakes. Our own Mauston has a secret recipe, and there is nothing equal to them, nothing at all. They are quite famous in town, I assure you."

"Are you acquainted with many poets, sir?" Althea said to John when Bella's attention had been drawn away by a question from Jane about the honey cakes.

"Scores of them. Poetry is quite the thing nowadays."

"Do you write poetry yourself?"

He reached for another honey cake. "When I have the time, you know. Been working on a sonnet, but now that the season's started, I shan't have more than a moment to myself, I dare say."

"And what is your sonnet about, if I may ask?"

He looked at her with real interest for the first time. "The legend of the men who turn into wolves by the light of the full moon."

"Oh my, very arresting. How did you come upon such a subject?"

"My friend Blakestone. He's an expert on the black rites of pagan peoples and has traveled absolutely everywhere. Even more than I have. That was before Bonaparte made it so damn difficult, you understand. Told me this story once about how he saw one of these men change into a giant wolf. That got me thinking of a sonnet."

"I should love to read it when you have it written."

"Thank you, cousin, but wouldn't it frighten you too much?"

"I am not so easily scared. Besides, there is something quite thrilling about the idea of wolves and moonlight."

John smiled, and Althea realized that he was actually even more handsome than he had first appeared. "Just so, dear cousin, just so," he said.

An hour later, the ladies of Dettamoor Park were finally released to their rooms to rest and then to begin the process of changing for dinner. They had been assigned connecting rooms on the second floor. After a brief toilette with the water basin and an hour of reading her volume on insects, Althea ventured to rap lightly on Jane's door.

"Come in," came the muffled reply. Althea pushed the door open.

Jane was seated primly in a chair. "I knew that you could not sit still for long."

"No, I could not. Besides, I was dying to hear your opinion of our cousins. Which have you selected as the companion of my future life?"

"John, of course. One shouldn't fall in love with the second son if one can help it."

"But I would have thought Charles was much more to your taste. Such respectability and prudence."

"Yes, he was very prettily behaved. He did me the honor of sitting by my side a full half an hour before he made his way to you. By the way, what could have kept you in such tight conversation with Lord Bingham? I don't know that I've ever seen such a strange, affected young man. And what, pray tell, was that thing wrapped around his neck?" Jane said.

"A neckcloth."

"A neckcloth? He looked like one of those hideous mummies."

Althea couldn't repress a giggle. "He fancies himself a poet, so you must make allowances. He's writing a sonnet about some legend that a friend of his swears is actually true."

"A legend about what?"

"Wolf men."

"My God. I am beginning to favor Charles. Give off thinking of the title. It's not worth putting up with such nonsense."

Althea sank down into the chair opposite. "It is not nonsense to him. And one might make allowances for a little folly in such a handsome man."

"Beauty fades soon enough. Don't bet your happiness on that."

"No, of course not. But you wouldn't wish me to marry a horror just for the sake of position." She paused and then added with feeling, "No matter how you approach the problem, I'm better off remaining free."

"I thought that too when I was your age, but I've had some years to reconsider."

"Surely you're not unhappy?"

"No indeed, but as one ages one feels the lack of a husband."

"And was there never anyone who made you wish to renounce your spinsterhood?"

"Oh, a great many, but all of them either objectionable to me or ineligible for a baronet's daughter."

Althea reached over and squeezed her hand. "We should be on the lookout for a husband for you."

"Fiddlesticks. Men my age have all lost their heads for chits out of the schoolroom."

"It is very provoking."

"Speaking as a former chit?"

Althea laughed. "It's not your age, Jane, but your tongue that will keep you single."

There was a discreet knock at the door. "Come in," Jane said.

Sally bobbed a curtsey. "Mrs. Buxton, that's her ladyship's own abigail, would be honored to attend your ladyship and Miss Trent's preparations for dinner."

Althea read Sally's petulant look. "One must allow Mrs. Buxton to try her hand if she is so keen. A refusal would be an insult of the highest magnitude. But you may certainly help us begin our preparations now, Sally. Please let Mrs. Buxton know that we shall require her services in an hour, perhaps?" Althea said.

Sally bobbed another curtsey and was gone again.

"We should have brought Dorkins with us," Jane said.

"The journey would have killed her. You know how she suffers with those spasms in her back."

"But it doesn't look right, you showing up without a proper abigail."

"It doesn't seem to have hurt me in Cousin Bella's eyes." Althea stood up. "Come Jane, I must have your opinion." They walked back into Althea's room. "Should it be the gray silk or that lavender crepe?"

"Neither. My God, Althea, we are in London now. You must and shall have a new wardrobe."

"What a task master! A stern face doesn't become you."

"If my face weren't stern, you would pay absolutely no attention to my advice."

"I tremble and obey."

"Of course you do. I have given it a great deal of thought, and I feel that it is time to have done with all of the black rigmarole."

"Perhaps that is not quite your decision, Jane dear."

"Of course it isn't, but if I don't push you, you'll never make one. I've been out of mourning a year now, and it is quite refreshing to be able to pick the colors that suit one."

"Lavender doesn't suit me?"

"Makes you a haggard wreck."

"Probably, but our circumstances are so different. You know our neighbors would have been quite shocked to see me lose the black so soon. A wife is not a sister, after all."

"There are no busybody neighbors here."

"Just all of London society."

"Since when have you cared about society? Don't tell me now that your scruples have taken over."

"You know that I have none. Well, this may come as something of a shock, but to please you, I think I can leave off the black bombazine while we are in town. I will have no experiments that require sturdy dresses, after all."

The news that Althea had decided on a new wardrobe sent Bella into an ecstasy of delight that was only restrained by the necessity of proceeding down to dinner. The honor of taking Althea's arm was awarded to the marquess. He was a stiff sort of gentleman, some years older than his spouse. He had once been a spitting image of his eldest son, but the years on the town were evident in the dark circles under his heavy lids and the multitude of wrinkles around his mouth. There was also a tension in the smile he bestowed upon her that made Althea wonder what trouble might lurk below his placid countenance.

"My dear, we are quite delighted that you have finally honored us with your presence. It is always amusing to have a pretty woman about the house."

"Thank you. You are too kind, Lord Levanwood." She met his gaze.

"Good. I thought you weren't one of those mealy-mouthed women who are too embarrassed to receive a compliment."

"One must take what one can get under the circumstances."

He chuckled as he handed her into the chair to his right. "Exactly so."

They were seated at a table that was too large for easy conversation with such a small family party. Instead, a stilted exchange in loud voices passed for polite communication. As Althea lifted her spoon to try the cream soup, the marquess said, "Sir Arthur Trent was enamored of scientific pursuits, I hear."

She swallowed quickly. "Why, yes. Before his passing, he was working collaboratively with Fellows of the Royal Society on a study of toads."

"He was a Fellow of the Royal Society himself, I understand."

"Yes." She took another sip of soup.

"I've had a new thought about my sonnet," John said to her.

She swallowed again and turned to him. "Indeed?"

Bella's voice came from across the table. "A ball, yes, we must have a ball!"

The marquess looked sternly at his spouse, but then turned back to Althea. "Toads. That is an interesting subject, I'm sure."

"The wolf man must transform by the light of the full moon. A large laughing moon."

"I've never had much experience with scientific men. Seen them about town, but nothing beyond that."

"The moon against the dark of the trees."

"A ball, yes! To launch dear Althea back into society. But there is so much to do. And she must have new gowns. Otherwise, what is the point?"

"I don't know that I could spend my time with toads. Slimy creatures. Although as a boy we used to have great fun putting them in our governess's bed."

"And I have spent some time thinking about the fur. I have to get the transformation from skin to fur just right, or it won't work."

"Dear Lady Trent would look lovely in blue, don't you think?"

"What about the phrase 'fur sprouting through the skin like new oats in a spring field'?"

"We had such larks as a boy. Crickets in the parlor. Mice in the schoolroom."

"And puce. There is nothing more elegant than puce for brown hair."

As the ladies recessed to the blue salon, Althea whispered to Jane, "I have never had a more tiring dinner in all my life! Even with three different conversations, I never got a word in edgewise."

Once the ladies were seated around the coffee, Bella grabbed Althea's hand and squeezed it repeatedly. "Oh, my dear cousin, I shall take you to Madame Longet first thing tomorrow, for she will know just what colors will set off your complexion. She's vastly expensive, but nothing is equal to her designs, absolutely nothing. Then we must call on Madame Harvey, for she fashions the most exquisite bonnets and lace caps, and you must be guided by her because, as we are cousins, I can be frank and tell you that the cap you have on now does not do your face justice. It quite swallows you up."

"I certainly do not wish to disgrace the name of Trent by appearing in society in an ugly cap."

"No indeed. One must look one's best at all times. And I will give you a piece of advice since you are new to town, and must be guided by me. There are certain ladies that you should take particular care to impress if you are to be well received by society."

"Indeed? Pray tell me their names so that I may be on my guard."

"The patronesses of Almack's for certain, although Lady Jersey is a particular friend of mine so you may rest easy in that regard. The Duchess of Richmond—"

"She isn't that Frenchwoman Richmond ran off with when I was in my first season, is she?" Jane said.

"The very same. Of course, now no one seems to remember the scandal. She is quite popular with the Prince of Wales, you see." Bella smiled.

"The prince always did have queer taste," Jane said.

"Be that as it may, you must not seek to antagonize her. No indeed. Or Lady Pickney either, come to think of it."

"Who is Lady Pickney?" Althea said.

"She's nothing to look at, and Lord Pickney isn't even very good ton, but that Pickney woman has the sharpest tongue in all of London. And what is worse, polite society seems to hang on her every word. It quite defies belief, but there it is. Do not get crosswise with her or you shall live to regret it. Why she said poor Charles looked like a fox about to steal an egg, and I tell you, what hope does he have of making a good match once that sort of thing goes around? It puts me all out of patience."

"Any woman with a good understanding will take such comments for what they are: silly chitchat," Althea said.

Bella sighed. "One can only hope."

Althea took another sip of coffee. "You mentioned the Duchess of Richmond. Word reached Somerset about some earrings of hers that may have been stolen. Do you know anything about that? Should I take special care with my jewelry here in town?"

"Oh yes, that was some time ago, wasn't it? Well, I will caution you because it appears that the thief who took her earrings is still at large. Not that you have anything to worry about in my household, for my servants are all to be trusted implicitly, but I do know several people who have suffered losses at this Richmond Thief's hand. Why, even Lord Belfore, who has been intimate with Lord Levanwood lo these twenty years or more, suffered the loss of a diamond brooch. The pity was that he'd laid out some monies several years ago to get it remade special for Lady Belfore to wear in her hair. It was a family piece, I believe. Ghastly looking thing, really, but Lady Belfore seemed fond of it."

"Oh dear," Jane said.

Althea opened her mouth to inquire further but was prevented from doing so by the entrance of the men. Indeed, Althea thought as she sipped her coffee, Cousin Charles did have the air of a fox about him.

CHAPTER THREE

The following morning they set out for Madame Longet's establishment, which was located in an elegant building on Bond Street. As an important customer, the Marchioness of Levanwood was ushered up immediately. She and her guests were asked to sit in a charming parlor and offered refreshment in the form of hot chocolate and sugared biscuits.

After several minutes, a small, dark lady with shrewd brown eyes swept into the room. "Ah, Lady Levanwood, how delighted I am that you have come." Madame Longet curtsied low and then said, "Please tell me how I might be able to serve you this morning?"

Bella quickly swallowed the other half of her fourth biscuit. "We have come for a new wardrobe for Lady Trent and Miss Trent, my cousins from Somerset, come to stay in London. As you can see, dear Lady Trent has been in mourning for my cousin but decided to put off the black and so must order some new dresses. And Miss Trent as well, for there is nothing like the London fashions."

"I see. Lady Trent, delighted to serve you. If you will permit, would your ladyship please stand?"

Althea complied.

"Ah yes, I think some of the new designs will suit your ladyship very well. Moderation in adornment is what is required for elegance this season. No girlish frills."

Lady Levanwood touched her lace collar self-consciously, but Madame Longet merely smiled. "And Miss Trent?"

Jane rose, and Madame Longet eyed her critically. "And I have just the style for a lady with such regal height. It will take the breath away. Lady Levanwood, Lady Trent, and Miss Trent, if you would please follow me into the salon."

Althea and Jane rose to follow. Bella hurriedly finished her hot chocolate and then bustled behind. The salon was furnished with several long tables. Four dress mannequins stood like soldiers at attention in the corners. The tables were covered with loosely bound dressmakers' fashion plates, some plainly engraved and others tinted by hand in watercolor, as well as sketches on loose paper, clearly the original designs of the establishment. There was a door to one side of the room that was partly open, and Althea spied shelves full of neat rolls of cloth to be shown to customers and heard the hushed murmur of Madame Longet's seamstresses.

"We have quite the latest prints available for review." Madame Longet gestured to the tables. "Although I would direct Lady Trent to this volume, as it contains just such a style as will suit to perfection." She pointed at a book lying open on the table close to the seamstresses' room. "And if you would permit me, I must confer with one of my staff a moment." She curtsied again and then slipped through the open door, closing it quietly behind her.

The ladies fanned out. Althea approached the selected volume and began to turn the pages slowly. Madame Longet was correct, these simple fashions were indeed just to her taste. Her eye settled on an evening gown of pale green satin with an unadorned square bodice, short puffed sleeves, and a fine net overskirt of silver threads, parted in the middle to show the satin. It would be just the dress to wear to a ball, and she had a lovely diamond set that Arthur had given her as a wedding present. She turned the page to examine a cambric day dress with a blue velvet spencer when her ear caught part of a conversation taking place behind the walls of the seamstress's workshop.

"And what are we to do with the bill, pray?" a voice said.

"We must act carefully, as it would not do to offend Lady Levanwood." That was definitely Madame Longet.

"Offend her? Why, I'd like to offend her. She hasn't paid for the last five gowns she ordered. Nor, given what I hear, is she like to."

"The Marquess of Levanwood will find a way. He always does," replied Madame Longet.

"You're a simpleton if you lend credit to her cousins. One spendthrift is like to travel with another."

"No doubt, but I shan't let them order more than a couple of gowns, no matter how many they desire. Then we shall see how quickly they pay. If that Lady Trent wishes to come out of mourning, she'll pay readily enough."

Althea heard the sounds of a hand on the doorknob and quickly shifted her focus back to the book of fashions.

If she could only have one or two dresses made, she should stick to the most important. One ball gown and one dress for supper would do as a start.

Several hours and numerous bolts of fabric later, Althea came away with an order for the green ball gown and a deep blue satin supper dress, cut low at the front and trimmed with worked Brussels lace. Jane escaped with a new printed cotton day dress and a fetching pelisse in dark green velvet. Lady Levanwood, after much back and forth, ordered nothing. Althea had to admire the deftness with which Madame Longet parried her client's insistence that nothing would do but to order another new dress for the as yet unplanned and unorganized ball.

However, that was put to rights, for as soon as the ladies reached the house, Bella said, "My dears, no matter what the marquess says, we must and shall have a ball. Why, I have that yellow silk gown that has never been worn. I ordered it too late last year to be of much use. For who wishes to wear a ball gown in the country? Summer is such a dull season, unless one can be by the sea, but the marquess was so disagreeable as not to follow the prince to Brighton. Some nonsense about economies and suchlike. It tries my patience to no end, but never mind because it wouldn't be right not to have a ball this season, for you are come and I have the dress. And the diamonds, of course. I will have Charles get them from the jeweler—loose stones you know—the setting is horrible, but they've been in the family for ages, and the stones are of the first water. The collar glitters like anything under the lights."

Bella then bustled away to begin the arduous task of writing out a list of potential invitees. Jane retired to her bedroom, and Althea took the opportunity to snatch a walk in the small back garden.

It wasn't much of a garden, just a square patch of dirt, planted with shrubs at the edges and the scraggly sprouts of new vegetables rising from raised beds grouped in the center. It backed up on the mews and was hemmed in by the other tall houses. The shrubs still bore evidence of frosty mornings, and the wisps of vegetable greenery were hardly picturesque, but any outdoor activity was preferable to yet another minute cooped up inside. Althea walked the length of the high wooden fence that enclosed the perimeter. There was a gate at one end, which she tried but failed to open. Presumably the staff had a key.

Even with the houses for a shield, she could still hear the rough sounds of the street. She had to admit that the noise unnerved her, and not for the first time she thought of the quiet of home. Or at least of a different kind of noise. Insects and birds and the rustle of the leaves in the trees. She reached out and touched the desiccated leaf of a boxwood bush, sliding the small waxy leaf between her fingers. Although the boxwood was known to repel insects, perhaps she might find one or two lurking about. She bent over to examine the shrub more carefully.

On the ground by the bush lay a dead raven. Arthur had once thought to do a study of ravens because he had observed enough of their behavior to realize that they were intelligent and organized animals. Given the lack of decay, Althea estimated that the carcass was only a day old. Althea touched the wing, shifting the bird. Several flies emerged from the bird's body and buzzed angrily. Althea grinned. Insects and a raven, two of Arthur's interests in one. Despite the lack of black dresses, she might just have to begin her observations anew. She turned the carcass over, observing other flies clinging to the raven's flesh. So quickly the predator became the prey.

"Roger?" A voice came from the stairwell down to the kitchen door.

Althea stood up quickly.

"Roger?" A man came up the steps. He was dressed in loose clothing and a long apron. "Oh, begging your pardon, milady. I thought you were Roger. I don't know where that boy's gone off to."

"I'm sorry, but he's not out here." She smiled. "Can I assume that you are the famous Mr. Mauston?"

He bowed his head sheepishly. "Yes, but not famous, milady."

"I'll be the judge of that. I've tasted those honey cakes, and even though Mrs. Huff has been the cook at Dettamoor Park for as long as I've been alive and would have my head for saying so, I can tell you that there is not a better cake around."

"Much obliged. I'm sure Mrs. Huff is quite a fine cook."

"Yes, good country food. But you have a way with supper that is altogether different. That soup last night was divine. Such a light touch with the cream, such a delicate flavor of watercress with the hint of sweet onion . . . but I'm rattling on when all you want is to find poor Roger. If he comes this way, I will send him back to the kitchen."

Mr. Mauston bowed again, this time bending at the waist. "Thank you very much, milady."

CHAPTER FOUR

Despite the marquess's objections, Lady Levanwood won the argument and cards for the Levanwood ball were sent around to all of the best families. The day of the event dawned fair and surprisingly mild. Lady Levanwood, perhaps to heighten the interest in her soirée, had kept Althea and Jane hidden away from a wider society than a couple of small parties could afford.

Madame Longet delivered Althea and Jane's dresses right on time and then several more once she realized how quickly Althea and Jane paid all of their bills. The Dettamoor Park ladies also found time to visit Madame Harvey. Althea was now the proud owner of several coal scuttle bonnets for daily use and enough delicate lace caps to last all season.

The house came alive with noise and excitement. Servants rushed to and fro carrying chests of silver and boxes of glassware. There were deliveries of every sort.

Althea could hear the stomp of boots up the back stairs and the murmur of voices. She donned an old gray dress and a new lace cap and sent Sally away as quickly as possible. The poor girl had been absorbed into the massive Levanwood workforce and looked so distracted that Althea pitied her. However delightful a ball was to the masters, the servants paid the price for so much frivolity.

Althea found Charles the only occupant of the breakfast parlor, but he hailed her with such good humor that she did not want for greater company.

"Cousin, I did not expect to find you dressed so early. I'm sure my mother must have kept you up half the night describing the anticipated glories of tonight's festivities."

Althea smiled and then selected a slice of ham from the chafing dish. "She did paint a delightful picture, but I am like the birds and cannot stand to miss the morning."

He seemed much struck by the remark. "We are of a common mind and shall be outnumbered in this family. Should you like a cup of hot chocolate? Here, let me pour you one."

"Oh yes, thank you." She sat across from him. "I presume that the rest of the family have not breakfasted yet?"

"Heavens no! Nor are they like to. One has to save one's strength for the dancing, you understand."

"Perfectly. But you do not dance?"

"Very poorly, I admit. Although I hope you will forgive the impertinence if I ask for the favor of a dance from you, Cousin Althea?"

"I'd be delighted. We shall be well matched, for I haven't danced above a dozen times since my marriage. Sir Arthur was not so fond of dancing, you see. In fact, I think he thought it a great waste of time." She took a sip of chocolate.

Charles hesitated a moment and then said, "I have always regretted the inability of our side of the family to—to maintain the proper connection with Sir Arthur."

Althea selected a slice of toast from her plate and spread it with marmalade. "I'm sure that you were not in a position to mend relations when the rest of the family was so violently opposed to our marriage." She looked steadily at him. "Or perhaps I should say, to me."

"No, cousin, surely—"

Althea laughed. "Don't bother to dissemble. Fortunately for me, my husband was brave enough to stand against the tide of outrage. Anyway, we lived so secluded that it didn't matter all that much."

"But, Cousin Althea—"

"Now things are different, are they not?"

He seemed relieved. "Yes, thank goodness."

Althea chewed slowly on a morsel of ham while Charles struggled to find another topic of conversation. Despite his smooth speech at their first meeting, closer acquaintance had revealed a reserved man sometimes awkward with conversation. Or at least, conversation with her. There was also an odd distance with Charles. However open and frank his manner, Althea could never quite be sure she knew exactly what he was thinking. Once or twice, she caught a strange expression in his eyes.

Althea swallowed. "Lady Levanwood told me your brother saw some action several months ago. He is in a Hussar regiment, I understand?"

"Yes. Augustus wrote a number of excited letters from a village in Spain. Skirmishes really, but very much to his taste. I couldn't have designed a better vocation for him than the army. He always was a crack shot and didn't care for books."

"And you have no taste for soldiering?"

He shook his head. "No indeed. It isn't in my nature to tramp about shooting at people. I much prefer my library."

"What sort of books do you read? I will own an eclectic taste myself."

"Histories and the biographies of great men, philosophers. My Latin and Greek are no more than tolerable, but I have a fondness for the classics. Homer in particular."

"So do I, although my father would be ashamed to see how poor my Greek has gotten of late. I find I do not have the time I once had to dedicate to study."

Charles almost dropped his fork. "You study Greek?"

"Studied. And Latin. My French is fair, but I got on quite well with Spanish and Italian. The German could be improved. It is such a guttural language, don't you think? It sticks in the back of the throat." Charles continued to stare, so Althea said, "As the only child of a learned physician, I was bound to absorb something from my father's daily conversation."

"It sounds as if you did more than absorb."

"Sorry to have shocked you, but as poor Papa had no son, what could he do but teach me? *Docendo discimus.*"

"You wrong me, cousin. I am not shocked, but pleasantly surprised." Yet there was something like wariness in the tone of his voice. "I had considered medicine at one point myself, you know. And I suppose I never thought to meet with such an accomplished female."

"Not accomplished, just extremely bookish. But don't tell Jane I said so, for she has told me that nothing will sink my credit faster than a reputation as a bookish woman."

Charles smiled conspiratorially. "So glad you are part of the family, dear cousin."

After a day of enforced confinement, the time finally drew near to stand at the top of the grand staircase to await the first guests. Althea arrived late after the prolonged ministrations of Lady Levanwood's abigail, Mrs. Buxton, who insisted that Althea adopt a fetching new hairstyle. Her hair was pulled to the top of her head and then ruthlessly curled with irons till it fell in delicate curls around her face. Mrs. Buxton had then affixed a silver net over the top knot and wound silver braid around it in the Grecian fashion. The confection was secured with a diamond pin. The pin formed part of the bridal gift from Sir Arthur that included the bracelet clasped gently around Althea's wrist and a fine pair of diamond earrings presently dangling from Althea's earlobes. As she was unused to wearing even this much, Althea declined the loan of further adornment from Lady Levanwood.

"Oh, my dear, how becoming!" Bella exclaimed upon seeing her. The marchioness was dressed in a satin gown of deep purple and a high turban of the same fabric that she had somehow managed to order from Madame Longet instead of the yellow gown from last season. Feathers sprouted from the turban like reeds in a marsh, and the famous Levanwood diamonds glittered at her throat. "I just knew Buxton would come up with the perfect solution for that straight brown hair of yours. Bewitching, don't you think, John?"

John seemed at a loss for words for a moment. Then he said, "Upon my word, it is. Devilish fine work, that Buxton. Why, I wouldn't be ashamed to be seen with you anywhere."

"Thank you, Cousin John, that is most obliging." Althea flushed in anger, but he seemed not to notice.

"Really, Althea, you look quite lovely," Charles jumped in apologetically.

The Marquess of Levanwood strolled into position beside his better half, who was more than a little annoyed at his tardiness. Althea, standing next to the marchioness, was privileged to witness some of the marital felicity of the Levanwoods.

"My Lord, so late! You drive me to distraction! Remember that this is a ball held at your house. Please do me the favor of attending to our guests properly instead of slipping off to play cards with your foolish friends," Bella hissed in his ear.

"I would not disparage my friends, madam, unless you examine the lot of flighty, empty-headed women you have designated as such. Your friends are what drive my friends away from these affairs."

Tears that may have been genuine sparkled on her lashes. "If you had any proper feeling, you would not tease me so. I warn you that I shall not be made a laughingstock yet again."

"As ever, that is entirely in your hands, my dear."

Bella opened her mouth to reply, but the sonorous voice of the butler announcing the first guest stopped her.

After an hour, Charles, John, Althea, and Jane were released to open the dancing and then attend to the guests in their own fashion. The rooms were quite crowded for an event so early in the season. After the obligatory country dance with Althea, John immediately disappeared, absorbed by the group of elegant young men who hovered just outside the card room. Charles guided Althea and Jane to a long bench already filled with the ladies who, by age or inclination, did not choose to dance. Jane, who had partnered with Charles, sank gratefully down, but Althea remained standing, unwilling for the moment to give in to fatigue.

"Cousins, may I get you some refreshment after the exercise of the dance? Lemonade?"

"Yes, thank you," Althea and Jane said in unison, and then they laughed.

Charles bowed. "Your wish is my command." He walked off in the direction of refreshment.

"Well, dear, tell me what you think of your first ball. Is it not delightful?" Jane said.

"I am duly impressed with both the room and the company. Really, some of the gowns here tonight are beyond description."

Jane caught Althea's inflection. "Indeed. The folly of fashion was always a great consolation to me in my time at the wall. However, I beg of you, do not think to engage in folly of any other kind. Bella warned me that the patronesses of Almack's are sure to make an appearance, as is Lady Pickney, who I suppose must be invited, damn the consequences. If you have any hope of catching the eye of an eligible party, you would be wise to mind your conduct."

"Poor Jane. I am such a trial for you, aren't I? But you need not worry about my manners, as I foresee many such evenings, attached like a pair of barnacles to the benches."

"Do you? We shall see. I've never seen you look better, by the way. That severe style suits you."

"And the deep rose of your gown brings color to your cheeks. It is quite becoming. Are you sure we hadn't better hunt for a husband for you, dear Jane?" Catching sight of a portly gentleman who seemed intent on reaching their section of the room, she added, "And here is one of your beaus, unable to resist such a vision in pink."

Jane rapped Althea's hand playfully with her closed fan. "Mind your manners, I said. Ah now, here comes Charles. When you have had your dance with him, I expect you shall not lack for partners."

To Althea's surprise, Jane was correct. After going down a set with Charles, she was handed off to a series of mostly agreeable men. Midway through the evening, Baron Casterleigh, a young man just back from university, led her through the steps of the cotillion. As Althea had previously only read about it in books, it took all of her concentration to watch the other couples and follow the baron's careful instructions. At the end of the dance, Casterleigh clasped her hand. "Well done, Lady Trent! No one would ever know that you had never danced it before."

"Thank you, Lord Casterleigh. It was your instruction that did it. I'm afraid I will never be able to replicate the feat."

"Then you must reserve all your cotillions for me."

"You are too kind." The musicians began tuning up for the next song.

Casterleigh seemed to recognize the tune and said, "I had not thought Lady Levanwood was quite so on top of the latest music."

"Dear me," Althea replied, unsure of what the next dance might be, "perhaps that is my cue to retire before my ignorance of the London fashions is more generally known."

"No indeed." Casterleigh touched the arm of a passing man. "I say, cousin, may I present you to Lady Trent. She's been hidden away in Somerset so long, she hasn't learnt 'La Boulangère.' But I can vouch that she is a capital dancer and would acquit herself well with an experienced partner such as yourself." He turned back to Althea. "Lady Trent, may I present my cousin, Duke of Norwich."

Norwich was a tall, fair man with a rigid bearing. He wasn't exactly handsome—his features being too harsh for such a compliment—but there was something about his face and figure that made Althea stand a little straighter in her satin slippers.

It was clear from the frown in Norwich's eyes that Casterleigh's claim upon his time was not welcome. However, good breeding got the upper hand, and he said, "Delighted to make your acquaintance, madam. Shall we?" He extended his arm.

Althea looked quickly around her, studying the couples who were just now taking the floor in circles of four couples each.

Norwich caught her hesitation and his face softened. "No need to worry, Lady Trent. I will tell you what you need to know."

His hand captured hers as they walked to their set. Althea felt an odd tingle at the base of her spine. Norwich smelled like clean linen and soap and some indefinable male cologne. She thought of several articles she had read on the use of smell in the mating rituals of animals. Then the music started in earnest, and she decided that studying the movements of the other dancers was more pressing than musing on animal behavior.

After guiding her along with precise directions for half the song, Lord Norwich said, "You are from Somerset, I understand."

"Yes. Lived there all my life."

"And you are staying here for the season?"

"Lord and Lady Levanwood were kind enough to invite me. My late husband was cousin to Lady Levanwood."

"I see. And how do you like London?"

"Quite well, although I feel I am more suited to country life. My husband's sister was mad to rejoin society, though, so Lady Levanwood's invitation was very much appreciated."

"I take it then that you enjoy all of the country pursuits—riding, walking, and the like."

"Walking, yes indeed. Jane says I'm a great walker, but riding is another matter. I am not a very avid horsewoman. A gentle pony is more than sufficient for my needs."

"And sufficient for a turn in Hyde Park. Therefore I think you will begin to prefer London."

"If you recommend it, it must be so." She looked up and caught a hint of a smile on his stern mouth. "But tell me, what do you pursue in London?"

He seemed surprised at the question, but replied, "The usual, I suppose. I ride in the park. I attend functions such as this. I manage the estates, and when I have a moment between letters and solicitors and whatnot, I read whatever book is to hand."

Althea drew him out about his literary tastes, and like all true book enthusiasts, his manner improved when it became clear that Althea was equally well-read and shared his opinions. When the dance ended, he said, "Lady Trent, you have no need to fear that your years in seclusion have impaired your ability to move in a more refined society."

Before Althea could thank him for such a compliment, however, she was accosted by Cousin John, come to claim another dance. Norwich bowed gracefully and withdrew.

"Got you out of that one, didn't I? Norwich is one of the stiffest, most deadly bores in all of England. I swear, I don't know what you found to talk with him about," John said.

Althea took John's arm. "Why, himself, of course."

CHAPTER FIVE

It was well past three in the morning when Althea finally found herself tucked in bed. Everything ached, but her eyes refused to close. Eventually, she got up, made her way through the dark, and rapped lightly on Jane's door.

"Come in," was the muffled reply.

Jane sat bundled in a shawl by the fire slowly dying in the hearth. "I knew you wouldn't be able to sleep."

"You either, I see."

"When have I ever been able to sleep?"

"You are like the creatures of the night, alive only by the light of the moon."

Jane smiled. "Come keep me company by the fire." Althea sat in the opposite chair. "Well child, you've done a good night's work. All the mamas of hopeful sons will be forcing their boys to send you flowers tomorrow, not the least of which will be Cousin Bella."

"Surely you jest."

"I am perfectly serious. Aside from the ability to laugh at the strange concoctions that pass for dresses these days—did you see that thing Lady Lamb had on, by the way, like a common—well, I was never so shocked—the wall has one other advantage."

Althea laughed. "And what is that?"

"Gossip. You probably did not realize it, but the fact that the Duke of Norwich favored you has done more to enhance your reputation than anything Cousin Bella could dream up."

"I danced with quite a large number of titled men."

"Indeed you did, but Norwich is known to be very rich and very particular in his choice of partners. He could have anyone, but he picked you. And for 'La Boulangère,' no less."

"Poor man, he couldn't get out of it. Lord Casterleigh practically forced him to dance with me. I was so tempted to laugh when I saw his face. He was not well pleased."

"Perhaps, but you must have grown on him. He seemed quite animated when he spoke with you."

"What reader is not passionate about books?"

"Oh, good heavens! Don't tell me you talked of books?" Jane started to laugh.

"It seemed a safe subject. Besides, my opinion was not required for much. He had very definite ideas."

"I'm sure he did, about you. He'll think you the worst sort of bluestocking if you keep on with your endless discussion of books and science."

"And what if he does? I did not find his company so delightful that I would wish to keep it," Althea replied.

"Be that as it may, a reputation for eccentricity will not win you any favors."

"Dear Jane, why do I think we have strayed into a conversation about your past?"

"Enough of your impudence."

"Then let us return to the gossip at hand. What else did you hear?"

"Nothing you or I wouldn't already know. The particulars of my brother's estate and your generous settlement were bandied about quite freely. Within the space of an hour, your circumstances were understood by all."

"The London crowd does move quickly. I assume that my previously humble origins were also known?"

"Not within my hearing. I think the quiet nature of your marriage may have prevented that news from traveling this far."

"Certainly a relief," Althea said.

Jane pointedly ignored her. "So given your current position as the widow of a baronet and the fact that Norwich has singled you out, I would say that you may aim as high as you please."

"London society is nothing more than a pack of dogs, I perceive. Where the lead dog goes, the others are sure to follow."

"As much as I deplore your analogy, you have the right of it. From what I have learned tonight, Norwich is the lead dog."

"And so I can have my pick of the seconds. Even Lord Bingham?"

"Yes. Although I can't imagine how you'd stomach a husband who slips out the back garden in the middle of the night."

"He does?"

"Several nights a week. At least it appears to be him. Probably off to meet some rake-hell friend. Other nights he just stands there, waiting for something or perhaps someone." She pointed to her window. "Stand over there and you can see quite a bit when the moon is high and the lamps are lit."

Althea moved to Jane's window and looked down. "Perhaps he seeks inspiration in the night sky for that sonnet of his. He's absent tonight, undoubtedly tired like the rest of us." Althea returned to her place by the fire.

"Not the marquess. In your whirl of activity, you may not have noticed how he stayed in the card room till midnight and then abruptly left the party in the company of several friends, including that Lord Belfore—the one with the stolen brooch. Bella noticed it, I can tell you. She looked ready to spit fire."

"So would I in her shoes. Although I have a feeling that Cousin Bella might overlook the fault if the marquess were lucky in his play."

"And why do you say that?"

"I overheard the dressmaker. Bella is deeply in debt to her, and a woman pays her dressmaker above anyone else. Then I heard a disparaging comment from Bella to the marquess. It has been my experience that a wife does not object to a husband's friends if she feels that they provide a beneficial influence. Add a love of cards to profligate friends and you have substantial gambling debts."

"A logical conclusion, I grant you. But the ton lives on debt in a way that you and I as country gentlewomen would find abhorrent. Even if money is to hand, they often will not pay their bills."

"Perhaps, but then Madame Longet would not be so eager to cut off an influential client. No, I feel the Levanwoods are in deeper than they would ever admit to you or me. Although, I do wonder how Cousin Bella managed to get Madame Longet to extend her credit for the dress she wore tonight and why the marquess let her give a ball in the first place. Then again, I suppose the ball had to be done or I might take offense, and that would not suit their purpose."

"Which is?"

"Did it not strike you as odd that persons who slighted me at my marriage now suddenly welcome my company?"

"Circumstances are different. Your position as a baronet's widow and the mother of the heir renders you entirely eligible for polite society."

"Yes, but this society? No Jane, it is too convenient. I am sure that Bella means to have me marry Charles, and I would imagine that the entrance on the scene of the Duke of Norwich has merely complicated matters."

The next morning, despite a great desire to sleep in, Althea arose with the birds yet again. She traveled down to the garden. After reviewing the insect depredations on the raven's corpse, she made her way back through the quiet house. It seemed clear that the servants were the only other persons ready to greet the day. The breakfast room was empty except for a kitchen maid who asked if she preferred chocolate or coffee. Althea chose chocolate and then served herself a fried egg.

She had just raised a forkful of egg to her mouth when she heard a sudden commotion coming from the hall. Althea got up and went to the door. The sound of running footsteps and hushed conversations were followed suddenly by the wail of someone crying. She flung the door wide and encountered a young housemaid frozen in place, her face white except for her bright red cheeks. She looked at Althea with a pair of large, frightened eyes and then put her hands over her eyes and sobbed.

"What, pray tell, is the matter?" Althea said.

The maid seemed incapable of speech.

"Come child, I don't bite. Is everything all right?"

The maid shook her head and continued to cry.

"Oh dear. I'm sure we'll set it all to rights. Come in here and tell me all about it." Althea took her arm and guided her into the breakfast parlor and shut the door behind her. Althea was sure that fraternizing with servants would not raise her social standing in London, but she did not hesitate to guide the maid to a chair and offer her a cup of cocoa from the pot. The poor girl looked positively wretched.

"Now drink some cocoa and stop crying long enough to tell me what's wrong."

The girl made a valiant effort to pull herself together, and then the words poured out like water. "The diamonds. Buxton done told me how to put them in the box just right. And I did, just like she told me to. Her ladyship even watched me do it, but Buxton don't believe me. She says I must have done something wrong and put them in the wrong place or worse, but, milady, I didn't. The case was open when I went in to see if her ladyship wished for something hot to drink. And the necklace was just gone. And now they've gone to wake the master and he'll be in a terrible rage and turn me off without a reference or send me to the noose. But you have to believe me. My mother raised me God-fearing, and

I'd never do such a thing, no matter what. I'm no thief!" She burst into another round of lusty tears.

"Pull yourself together," Althea said gently. "I'm sure no one thinks you stole anything. Just tell me again what you did last night with the necklace."

The maid hiccupped. "I put it back in its case just like her ladyship told me to. Then I closed the case and locked it. Her ladyship told me to leave it on her dressing table, so I did. I helped her ladyship dress for the night and get into bed. Then I drew the curtains round the bed and blew out the candle."

Before Althea could reply, the door swung open, revealing the imposing figure of Mrs. Buxton. "There you—" She stopped and looked at Althea. "Lady Trent. Oh my!"

Althea intervened. "Mrs. Buxton, I hear the house is in some confusion this morning. Lady Levanwood has misplaced her necklace?"

"Yes, Lady Trent. We are searching for it now." Buxton looked at the maid. "Mary, you are wanted upstairs."

"I don't know that Mary will be much help in this case. I rather suspect that it is not lost. In fact, someone knows exactly where it is. Has Bow Street been called?"

"Not yet. Lord Levanwood ordered a search of the house first."

"By all means, but let us not lose precious time. Was the lock on the case broken?"

Mrs. Buxton nodded. "The lock was forced open."

"Um. However, I still think that this may be the work of the Richmond Thief. And if that is the case, Mary will be of no use to anyone either here or upstairs."

Two hours later, the marquess must have decided to agree with Althea's assessment because Althea saw an underservant slip out through the back garden and run off down the street. By noon, Althea heard the door open and voices in the hall. She caught the low rumble of Magistrate Read. "Ah yes, I fully comprehend. If your lordship would be so kind as to give me the use of a room, I may begin the interviews while my principal officers, Mr. Standon and Mr. Lavender, commence a search of the premises."

Not wanting to cause further inconvenience, Althea repaired to her room, but she noted in passing that the hall seemed strangely full of flowery bouquets. Those couldn't really be for her, could they?

Half an hour later, Sally rapped softly at her door. "Mistress, there's a gentleman in the red salon what desires to speak with you." Sally's eyes were wide with excitement. Certainly, they had never had cause to summon Bow Street to Dettamoor Park.

"Thank you. I will be down directly."

Mr. Read was leaning against a marble fireplace when Althea entered, staring down into the newly banked fire as if searching for answers, his hand working at the crumpled folds of his cravat.

"Ahem." Althea gently cleared her throat.

Mr. Read looked up with a start. "Oh, Lady Trent, I did not hear you come in."

"My father always likened me to a cat."

Read smiled. "An admirable quality." He gestured at one of the chairs pulled up to the fire. "Please come and sit. My questions will not take you away from your other amusements for long."

"On the contrary, I believe your inquiries will be far more amusing to me than any of the other occupations I may pursue today." She sat down.

"Perhaps they may." He sat down in the opposite chair. "You know, I find it a great piece of luck that we should meet again, Lady Trent."

"Even under such circumstances?"

"Especially under such circumstances. I was much struck, your ladyship must understand, by the tone of our prior conversation. If I may say so, it is rare to meet with anyone, man or woman, with such quickness of mind."

"Mr. Read, you flatter me beyond my just desserts."

"No indeed. Am I correct in thinking that your father endeavored to give you the education that he himself possessed?"

"Did you know my father?"

"By reputation. Dr. Claire was quite a renowned physician in his day."

"I see the Richmond Thief is not the only subject of your investigations."

"Merely a few inquiries to satisfy my own curiosity. I apprehend his practice was centered in and around Taunton, but that he was consulted by the London practitioners."

"He was highly skilled in treating afflictions of the lungs and bad humors of the blood."

Read nodded. "I have been rightly informed by my sources as to your father, but your ladyship remains a mystery."

"Let me save you the trouble of further investigation. My father gave me an education that was unusual for my sex and age, but then we were very close, and I had no mother to chide him into a proper course. I did study medicine and assisted him as best I could, but I fear I never achieved his brilliance. Medicine is an art, you understand, and the best practitioners have a certain knack that cannot be taught."

"I see."

"In any case, my formal studies ended with my marriage to Sir Arthur Trent."

"Sir Arthur was some years your ladyship's senior, I believe."

"Yes, he was only several years younger than my dear father. And to prevent you from inquiring further, I will add that he was a patient of my father's. My father took me along to attend him during a particularly vicious spring cold. One is to suppose that Sir Arthur fell in love with my beauty, but I have never been a romantic. It was more that he sought a partner with an equal interest in science and, as no other suitable party had ever appeared, determined to make an offer to me."

"Again, I fear your ladyship is too modest."

"Fiddle. Now, sir, please let us get to the matter at hand. I am all interest. Does the disappearance of the Levanwood diamonds have anything to do with the Richmond Thief, do you think?"

"What is your ladyship's thought?"

"That it seems to loosely fit the mold."

"That is my conclusion as well."

"But perhaps we could be too hasty. My father instructed me never to jump to conclusions too precipitously, but rather to examine all of the facts first."

Mr. Read smiled. "A wise maxim to be sure. And what other facts does your ladyship wish to examine?"

"Why do I feel that this interview has less to do with the missing gems and more with an illustration of my character?"

"Perhaps I should be clear about my intentions. Bow Street works with very limited resources and must take every advantage available to us. My principal officers are fine men, but they can never have access to all of the relevant information."

"You desire my assistance to locate the diamond necklace?"

"If your ladyship would deign to assist us, we would certainly be most grateful. I promise that any communication would be kept confidential."

"How delightful!" Then she looked down. "Perhaps that was not the most ladylike reaction, but I will admit to you that the life of idle dissipation does not suit me."

"I had hoped not. Should your ladyship fear for your safety, I must hasten to add that Bow Street has several well-placed persons who also assist us from time to time because they have access to social circles that my Bow Street Runners cannot hope to enter. With your permission, I will ask one of these agents to contact you. He has been working on the problem of the Richmond Thief for some time now and should welcome the assistance. I assume that Lady Levanwood has made inquiries for vouchers to Almack's? It is soon to open."

Althea nodded. "She procured a voucher for me from Countess Jersey. We mean to attend next week."

"Perfect. I will have my agent contact you then. You shall know him by the word *butterfly*."

Althea smiled. "Given my interests, that is most appropriate."

Mr. Read rose as if to escort her to the door, but Althea protested, "Magistrate Read, please, we must follow protocol. I will now describe for you my movements since I last saw the diamonds around the marchioness's neck and give you any other information at my disposal."

He sat back down and withdrew a small pad of paper from his breast pocket and a well-worn pencil. "I see you know my duty better than I do."

Althea gave him an arch look. "One day I hope to."

CHAPTER SIX

That Wednesday evening, Althea dressed with more than special care in a dark blue satin gown with point lace at the collar and covering the puffed sleeves. She had just ordered it from Madame Longet, and that lady, happy to indulge a prosperous patron, had delivered it with extraordinary speed.

How silly, Althea thought to herself as Mrs. Buxton again appeared to perform her miraculous ministrations, *that an assignation with an agent of Bow Street should supply me with greater excitement than the flower of London society.* But so it was.

Jane had called her distracted that afternoon over tea, but in reality her thoughts were highly focused on a single question. Who was to be the mysterious agent? She imagined him tall and dark, with keen eyes and a brilliant mind. He must be confident and cunning and possess a smooth charm, which allowed him to blend easily into every society. Highborn, but not so high that he was unused to doing for himself. Well traveled and a master of languages. And disguise. One must not forget the art of the chameleon. In sum, a man who combined perfect intellect with all of the finer points of character and beauty. A prince among men. And just the man, if one were willing, to tempt a widow woman from her contented solitude.

Buxton tugged at her hair, and the vision of Prince Charming vanished into thin air. Althea eyed her reflection in the mirror. Buxton pulled again, braiding her hair on both sides and bringing it up into a twist high on the back of her head with a band of point lace wrapped around it as a nod to Althea's matron status. This time there were no soft curls to frame her face. Instead a yellow rose was placed just behind her ear in the Spanish style—a rose from one of the many bouquets that had indeed been sent in honor of her entrance into society. Althea wasn't sure whether to laugh or cry, but she'd picked the yellow rose because it was common enough among the bouquets to minimize the chance of raising a single gentleman's hopes.

When she descended the stairs to be handed into the family carriage by Charles, he met her with yet another expression of approval. "That color does favor you, Cousin Althea."

"Thank you, Charles. Sir Arthur always liked this color."

The mention of her departed husband seemed to stop any further effusions. Jane met her eyes ruefully but refrained from comment. The small group ascended to the confines of the Levanwood carriage, Lord John and the marquess having declined to partake of the country dances and lemonade offered by Almack's assembly rooms.

The rooms at Almack's were elegant in their simplicity. Not so the fashionable crowd that had assembled under the candlelight of the crystal chandeliers. Althea marveled at the profusion of satins and the glitter of gems. Plumes rose to the ceiling from enormous turbans, some so tall that Althea feared the risk of fire from a stray drop of sizzling wax. Perhaps the Richmond Thief would make another attempt, although stealing a bauble from the wearer in situ did not seem to be part of his plan. In any case, Althea looked around her anxiously for anyone who might be the Bow Street agent.

"Norwich hasn't arrived yet, my dear," Jane said dryly.

"What makes you think I am looking for him?"

"You should be. Another night like the night of the ball and you will be the toast of the town."

"As if that mattered."

"Then whom are you so arduously seeking?"

"Was it that obvious? I should learn to be more subtle if I am to get on."

Jane laid a hand on her arm. "Get on with what? You've been acting strangely. What are you hiding from me?"

Althea hesitated a moment and then whispered in Jane's ear, "I promise to tell you everything tonight, but for now just let me find my way. I am looking for someone I've never met."

"Never met? Really Althea, you are just talking nonsense now. Besides, you must wait for Lady Jersey to introduce you to a gentleman not already known to you. Ah, good, here she comes." Jane looked over at an imposing woman, trussed up like a turkey in a low-cut gown of green satin and egret feathers, slowly making her way over to their party.

A small, portly man trotted at her heel. Althea recognized them from the Levanwood ball.

"My, the years have not been kind to her," Jane added under her breath.

"Who is the gentleman, again? I have forgotten his name," Althea said.

"Sir Neville Tabard, a great friend of the Duke of York. He's quite got on since I knew him last."

Althea gave Jane a speaking look, but then Lady Jersey was upon them.

She embraced Lady Levanwood warmly. "Oh my dear child, such news about your lovely diamonds! When I heard what happened, I positively burst into tears. I truly did. They are saying it was that Richmond Thief again! Such a terrible thing, and Bow Street seems powerless to stop the man. How can any of us feel safe with such a brute roaming large?"

"Upon my soul, I've never been so shocked in all my life," Sir Neville said, waving an oversize quizzing glass strung on a satin ribbon around his neck dramatically in the air. "Why, to think he might have killed us all as we danced!"

Althea had to repress a smile. "Fortunately, he seems not to have added murder to his other crimes."

"Ah yes, quite true," Sir Neville said. There was a pause in the conversation.

Lady Levanwood wrung her plump hands together and sought to fill the void. "Lady Trent, I believe you know Sir Neville Tabard."

Althea extended her hand, and he grasped it lightly and then bowed low. Althea heard the creak of a corset and the jangle of the various fobs and seals Sir Neville found indispensable to carry on his watch chain. "Delighted."

Althea bobbed a curtsey. She could hear the sound of the musicians tuning up, signaling the start of the dancing. Althea caught Charles's eye. He'd expressed a wish of dancing the first with her.

"Lady Trent," said Lady Jersey, "I've observed that you are not averse to dancing. May I present Sir Neville as a desirable partner for the set that is just forming?"

"Of course." Althea gave Sir Neville a formal smile.

Charles graciously stepped back. Sir Neville extended his arm, and Althea laid her hand upon his sleeve.

As the set came together, Althea remarked, "It is delightful to meet Jane's former acquaintance. I find myself quite curious as to her life prior to her retirement into Somerset. Is she much changed?"

"No indeed. I was immediately struck with how little time has etched her features. I would have known her in an instant," he said warmly.

"In her mind as well as her person?"

"Yes. Although we had but little speech at Lady Levanwood's ball, she appears to be what she always was—a lively wit."

"Perhaps that is why she and I have always maintained such warm relations."

The line formed, and Althea executed the first pass. When she came back around, Sir Neville seemed anxious to change the conversation. "And how do you find London, Lady Trent?"

"Very well. I have become quite frivolous."

"It is not frivolity to enjoy the delights of refined society." He executed a turn. "For all of his ungainly roundness, he was quite an elegant dancer.

"You must know best. I have been isolated at home for too long to be able to judge."

She moved down the line, and then they came back together. "I find it hard to believe that this is your first season, so to speak. If I may be permitted, your dancing does your dancing master credit."

Althea smiled. "As I've had none, I will take that as a credit to my own ingenuity or your skills as a partner."

"What? No dancing master? Surely Lady Levanwood, knowing how you were situated, must have made arrangements."

"Please do not blame Lady Levanwood. She offered, but so far I have not felt the need to accept."

"There is no need—" He moved away again and Althea waited patiently until he came back around. "Your ladyship has the grace of a butterfly flitting from flower to flower."

Althea hesitated, momentarily stunned. "You, sir?"

"Have I said something amiss?"

"No. Very prettily said. And so how shall we proceed?"

"Well, this turn is followed by a pass through and then your ladyship takes my hand—"

"Not the dance, the Richmond Thief. What shall we do?"

"Why, lock up your jewels, to be sure!"

"Besides that. Mr. Read said you would have some instructions for me."

Sir Neville moved away from her, a puzzled look on his face. Althea watched him, unsure of her next move.

"Instructions? I am a sad rattle to be sure, but I'm afraid I haven't followed your ladyship's conversation. Of what were we speaking?"

"I don't know," she replied, conscious that she had made a very great mistake. "Of the dance, I believe."

The next dance was claimed by young Casterleigh and another by an officer Althea had met somewhere before, but couldn't quite remember, and then finally Cousin Charles was able to cut in before a dashing Conde de Zaragoza carried Althea off for a country dance.

"Would you prefer some refreshment to dancing?" he said.

"Yes, thank you. I had not realized what healthful exercise dancing could be." They walked through the crowd to the supper rooms, where the press of people had grown to shocking proportions. If this was the start of the season, Althea was not sure she wanted to see the season in full swing.

Charles slowly moved his way through the mass of people, nodding here and there to acquaintances. When they had reached the refreshment tables, he said, "You seem to enjoy dancing."

"I find I do indeed enjoy it. Such a pity that Sir Arthur did not have the inclination. I think he would have liked it had he persevered in the attempt."

"You still mourn him often, I believe. Cake?"

"Thank you, no. All the more so when it comes upon me unawares. Amazing how little things can hold such memories."

Charles handed her a cup of lemonade. "Your grief does you credit."

"No more than my husband deserved." The lemonade was watered down, but refreshing nonetheless. Althea continued to examine the crowd, looking for her Bow Street agent.

"Sir Arthur Trent was very fortunate. Would that I had such luck."

Was that a declaration? Already? She pretended not to hear. "Shall we go back, do you think? I am promised for the set after next."

He swallowed the last of his lemonade. "I do not wish to keep you from your appointed dance."

An hour later, Althea was no closer to knowing the identity of her agent than she had been before. She sat down next to Jane, determined not to be tempted out to the floor for at least the space of two dances so that she could catch her breath.

"It looks like you didn't need Norwich again, my dear," Jane said.

"Which just proves that every man is mad for money, or that eccentric, scientifically minded females are all the rage in London."

Jane laughed. "Or both. That conde you were dancing with two dances ago had quite an air about him."

"And quite an accent. I am afraid that I was soon forced into Spanish. His English was absolutely unintelligible."

"Oh dear. Was he impressed or horrified?"

"Hard to tell with those black brows and that mustache. He told me my eyes were like *la luz del amanecer.*"

"And what, pray tell, does that mean?"

"Why, the light of the dawn, of course."

Jane made a sour face. "Rubbish!"

Althea laughed. "The Spanish are quite extravagant in everything. I'm sure such a compliment is equivalent in English to *how do you do.*"

"It makes Cousin John seem normal."

"I have come to understand that poetry is not just the province of the foreign exiles. More than one of my English partners has quoted verse to me," Althea said.

"We are living through a dissolute age."

"Ah, here comes Sir Neville. He certainly won't offend your sensibilities with verse."

"Ladies," Sir Neville began, "I have come to tell you what a charming picture you make—a delightful tête-à-tête. May I join you?" He indicated an open space of bench beside Jane.

"Of course," Jane replied.

He sat down with a creak of whalebone and a jangle of fobs. Then he produced a large white scented handkerchief and mopped his brow with delicate precision. "Such crowds. Such heat. I had not thought the season so far advanced. How do you like Almack's, Lady Trent?"

"Quite well, thank you," Althea replied.

"And you, Miss Trent?"

"It is much as I remember it, although not comparable to the Pantheon in our day."

Sir Neville's eyes lit up. "Yes indeed. Do you remember that great domed hall? Like a grand church it was. Mr. Wyatt's best work."

"I agree entirely." Then Jane seemed to notice Althea's inquiring look. "It burned down in my first season. The place they have now may share the name but is nothing to it."

"Nothing at all," Sir Neville said. "How grand I felt, Lady Trent, a young buck out on the town with my silks and velvets, promenading through the Pantheon's great rotunda." He looked at Jane. "The finery of today is plain by comparison with what we wore then, is it not, Miss Trent?"

Jane smiled. "True sir. I had some very fine stiff voile gowns, I remember."

"A rose velvet gown with silver lacing, and that garnet set done up in your loose, powdered hair," Sir Neville said suddenly, as if catching after a long buried memory.

"I did have such a gown," Jane replied, surprised.

"Powder?" Althea said.

Jane chuckled. "Yes, dear. It was quite the thing, I assure you! I had mine scented with lavender and wore it just as Sir Neville has described, dusting my long, curled locks."

"A siren in pink," Sir Neville added gallantly.

"I will have to trust your collective memories, for I'm afraid I cannot form such a mental picture."

"I have some of the gowns tucked up in trunks at the park. I'll show you when we return to Somerset," Jane said.

"Please, no talk of Somerset when you are so delightfully ensconced in the bosom of society," Sir Neville said.

"Have you no love for the country, Sir Neville?" Althea said.

"Oh, I like it well enough in August when London becomes like a furnace. Ranleigh House is situated in Devonshire."

"I have often heard Devonshire praised as one of the most beautiful locations in England," Althea said.

"It is. You both must visit Ranleigh when the season ends."

Althea looked at Jane for guidance, but Jane merely bowed her head and said, "You are too kind, sir."

"No, you must. For even Lady Pickney was so kind as to say that nothing compared to the gardens of Ranleigh."

"Lady Pickney is well known for her wit, I understand," Althea said.

"Have you made her acquaintance?" Sir Neville said.

"Yes, Jane and I met her at the Levanwood ball, but only briefly. I have been told that I must make a good impression with her to get on in society, but I have no way of knowing what she might have thought of me."

"No impression is likely as good as anything," Jane added.

Sir Neville smiled and nodded. "Miss Trent has the right of it, as always."

"Lady Trent, may I have this dance?"

Althea's head whipped around. Norwich stood in front of them, a hard expression in his gray eyes.

"I'm sorry, sir, but I am promised to Lord Baldwin for the next set. I am free the one after."

"Then perhaps you would be so kind as to accompany me for some refreshment?" He said it as a command rather than a wish.

"Yes, thank you." She stood and extended her gloved hand. He took it lightly in his own. "But you'll find the supper rooms quite crowded at the moment."

"Never mind," he replied brusquely, and he walked quickly away, trailing Althea.

But instead of leading her in to supper, he turned, opened a door, and ducked into a small chamber apparently utilized for storage. Althea followed, but she regretted it when he shut the door behind her. In the dim light that filtered from under the door, Althea could see shelves along two walls and crates of glasses and plates pushed up against a third.

Althea backed as far away from him as she could. "Sir, why have you brought me here?" She had on occasion read novels that talked of ruthless villains who preyed upon innocent females, but she had never thought to meet with one herself. She had to admit that the idea had a certain thrilling aspect.

Norwich's grim expression did not change. "Butterfly," he said slowly.

Althea stared back at him. "You? But how—why?"

"I could ask you the same thing. Read must be soft in the head to think that you would—"

"To think that I—what?"

"Forgive me, madam, but to ask you to help Bow Street."

Norwich's tone of voice was so condescending that Althea immediately felt the anger well up inside her. Her mind replayed the thousand petty slights and injustices she had suffered in her seven and twenty years. Men like Norwich always thought their understanding superior to hers. It was beyond provoking! "Why shouldn't he ask me to help?"

"And what could you possibly do that would be of any use? What could any woman do to help in such a case?"

Althea pulled herself up as straight as possible. "So you object to my sex?"

"I'll admit that you seem intelligent enough, but delicately bred females are not meant to go chasing after thieves and assassins—it offends all sensibilities. Surely you must see that."

"I do not see that. And why should I?"

Norwich threw up his hands. "Because no woman is clever or educated enough for such cunning work!"

"Neither my father nor my husband found fault with my education, so why should I admit fault to you?"

"What husband isn't blinded by the sight of a pretty wife? And who was your father? I've never encountered so much nonsense before in my life."

Althea's voice dripped with venom. "My father was Dr. William Claire, sir. A physician above all physicians in understanding, insight, and knowledge and one of the greatest minds of his generation. I'll thank you not to malign his memory."

"Oh, for the love of all that is holy!" Norwich reached out as if to grab her by the shoulders, but she evaded his grasp.

"I would not mention religion at such a moment, else you will force me to remind you that the meek shall inherit the earth. Now do step aside so that I may end this distasteful interview!"

He paused, suddenly conscious of the seething wrath that reddened Althea's cheeks and made her heart race. "Forgive me, I've let my tongue get away with me, but I merely—"

She stamped her foot, cutting him off. "Move, sir, or I will be forced to scream at the top of my lungs."

He stared at her, and she gave him back stare for stare. Finally, he stepped to one side, and she opened the door with a flourish. "I hope Your Grace will not take offense, but I sincerely wish that we shall not meet again. *Cessante causa, cessat effectus!*" Then she pulled the door shut behind her.

CHAPTER SEVEN

Althea was unusually silent in the carriage on the return to the house. Cousin Charles tried by means of lighthearted teasing to bring her out, but he failed in the attempt. When the women retired to their chambers, Jane lost no time in coming into Althea's room. Althea was seated at her dressing table, angrily running a brush through her long chestnut hair and staring at her reflection in the glass.

"What happened to you tonight?" Jane crossed her arms. "And I will not leave until you give me the whole story."

Althea sighed. "You won't be happy about it."

"I had deduced as much already."

Althea pulled the brush ruthlessly through another lock. "Well, at least I shan't be bothered by Norwich again." She met Jane's worried gaze in the mirror. "Sit down, dear. This may take some time."

Half an hour later, Jane said, "All in all, it is not as bad as I feared, and so long as this doesn't go farther than this room, it may all come out right. Norwich has done enough that it is of little matter if he never speaks to you again."

"I hope he doesn't speak to me again! Odious creature. But what's to be done about the investigation? How am I to help Magistrate Read if Norwich will not assist me?"

"The investigation?" Jane said indignantly. "You seriously propose to assist Bow Street?"

"Of course! You do not think that Norwich's paltry arguments would put me off, do you? A criminal is at large, and Bow Street may never be able to gather all of the information it needs to catch him."

"I should have expected as much," Jane said ruefully. "Arthur always said you were like a dog with a bone when you got some fool idea in your head."

"Is it foolish to think that a woman may be smarter than a man? Why, we have only to look at the animal kingdom to see that it is often the female of the species who rules the colony. Think of the bees, Jane, or the mantis, or the—"

"You'll be the death of me yet."

"You're healthy as a horse, and you know it. But what is to be done?"

Jane sat in silence for a minute, and then her broad mouth cracked a wicked smile. "Why, investigate the matter ourselves."

Althea stood up and embraced Jane. "Thank goodness! I knew you would not fail me."

The next morning, Althea got up early and, after a visit to the raven in the back garden and a light breakfast, made her way to the library. Lady Levanwood preferred to write letters in her room, so she had granted Althea the use of her small feminine desk under a window. Althea took full advantage of the morning sunlight to pen her letters and note her observations of the maggots, flies, and now the spiny larvae of her beloved beetles feasting on the raven's corpse. *Dermestes trentatus* was particular in its choice of food, preferring desiccated flesh to other alternatives.

Although Sir Arthur had outlined the beetle's life cycle in his copious notes, Althea hoped that her recent observations might lead to a novel path of inquiry. Then she would have what she needed for a first-rate publication, assuming, of course, that she could find a way to convince the Royal Society to publish it. Althea smiled to herself as her nimble pen traveled across a fresh sheet of paper. Jane sought to remove Althea from scientific temptation here in London. How little Jane knew of Althea's scientific interests.

When Althea finished with her insect observations, she turned her attention to her letters. Yesterday afternoon, Althea had a received a letter from her son's tutor that enclosed another short epistle from her son himself, and so she desired to reply as soon as possible. Although Althea had feared that motherhood would not agree with such a scientifically minded female, one look at her son's little red face had reassured her that a mother's love would not be alien to her practical soul. And as she gazed at the awkward writing, she felt overwhelmed with a longing to be with him once again.

She drew a sheet of the Levanwood paper toward her and hesitated only a moment before her pen flew on in loving endearments and encouraging questions about the progress of his studies. In fact, she was so engrossed in an inquiry about Latin grammar that she did not hear the door open.

"Ahem," a soft voice said behind her. She looked back with a start. A liveried footman stood in the doorway with a silver tray. "This just came for your ladyship," he said.

Althea got up and inspected the tray. A flat white envelope lay precisely in the middle. On the envelope were the words "Lady Trent" and nothing more. The handwriting was unfamiliar to her.

"Thank you." She took the envelope.

The servant bowed and then exited the room, closing the door behind him. As soon as he was gone, Althea turned the envelope over to inspect the red wax seal. Some sort of figures, perhaps the three graces, but nothing that identified the owner. She broke the seal and walked back to the desk to spread the sheet flat and examine it in the light of the window.

In very precise handwriting was scrawled the following:

I have come to regret my actions. Would that you could forgive the same. If so, please come to Hyde Park at half past five o'clock. If I do not see you, I shall know your answer.

N.

"Well, well," Althea muttered, "I wonder if Mr. Read gave him a talking to? Then again, I suppose a duke may do anything he likes, so perhaps the contrition is genuine."

There was a knock at the door, and Althea hastily shoved Norwich's note under her own incomplete missive. "Come in."

Charles stepped into the room. "Ah, cousin, I thought to find you here."

"Yes, your mother has been kind enough to let me use her writing desk. I received a note from my son, you see."

"How delightful. And what does he write of his progress?"

"It seems his studies are well advanced. At least that is what I gather from him and the letter that accompanied it from Mr. Pellham. We have high hopes that young Arthur will be every bit the scholar that his father was."

Charles smiled. "And his mother."

"You are too kind." Althea crossed the room and sat down in a chair that was pulled up to the fire.

Charles sat opposite. "No, I think not."

There was an awkward silence. Charles rubbed his hands together nervously.

Then Althea said, "And how is Lady Levanwood taking the shocking theft of her diamonds? She seemed in good spirits last night, but such a loss must be very difficult to bear."

"She feels it more than she would let on to us. That necklace has been in the Levanwood family for many generations."

"The diamonds were stunning, to be sure. But I wonder how the word of her choice to wear them could have gotten out. Surely only the family would have known?"

Charles coughed. "Pardon, but perhaps you have not been in London long enough to know that nothing may be kept quiet. One has only to look at the staff of any great house to see that the number of persons who may have knowledge of such a thing is endless. And then there are the bankers and the jewelers, and so on."

"Surely you do not suspect the bank? And the jeweler would have no reason to steal a piece as well known as the Levanwood necklace."

"Who is to know what the motive was?"

"Money, I suppose. Forgive my impertinence, but I do hope the necklace was insured."

Charles nodded. "Let us not talk of such distasteful subjects." He stood abruptly. "Lady Trent, Cousin Althea, I think you may have guessed the reason for my seeking you out this morning."

Althea stared at him, a dull ache starting in the pit of her stomach. "No, I'm afraid not, Cousin Charles."

He started to pace, muttering to himself. "Surely, but perhaps I spoke too soon. In any case, my feelings will be denied no longer." He stopped and placed a hand over his heart. "Dearest Althea, would you do me the great honor of becoming my wife?"

Althea looked down, unsure of how to answer such a declaration. The Levanwoods must be in dire straits to force the issue so soon. "I—sir—cousin." She cleared her throat and looked up. "I'm sorry to pain you, but I had not thought—I was not contemplating—in short, I cannot accept your generous offer."

He looked crestfallen, but then he said solemnly, "I fear I have been too precipitate. Your grief for your late husband does not abate sufficiently to allow you to entertain the offer of another."

Althea jumped at the excuse. "Yes. I have just now put on colors, and I cannot contemplate marriage with anyone until my heart—Sir Arthur's death was a great blow to me. I do not feel fully recovered."

Charles bowed low. "I honor your sentiments, cousin, more than words can say." He took her hand and kissed it reverently. "But I do hope that in time you will consider my offer. My heart shall remain yours until you chose to claim it." Then he bowed again and swiftly left the room.

Althea stared at the fire, trying to catch her breath. Her heart raced—not with excitement but with anxiety. How could Charles have thought she was ready for such a step? And if Charles was not solely motivated by money, then had she done anything to lead him to believe that she would welcome his advances? She could think of nothing, except that her generally open and unguarded temperament may have led her astray. She must try to be as aloof as the London women pretended to be.

And there was the Norwich matter to be taken care of as well. Somehow she had to convince someone to take her to Hyde Park, since young ladies, even widowed ones, did not venture forth without accompaniment. This might have proved an easy task had she shown any prior inclination to promenade with the town notables farther afield than Grosvenor Square. Instead, she had declined any number of offers to accompany Lady Levanwood. But perhaps she could convince her hostess that the allure of Hyde Park was too great to resist, even for Althea, and endeavor to meet Norwich without raising suspicion.

Althea went to the desk and refolded the note, slipping it again under her own letter, and finished her missive. She gathered up her papers, determined to work on the monograph when her mind was more settled, and then thought better of leaving. The Levanwood's library had clearly been assembled by a notable reader sometime in the last century. However, as to new volumes, it lacked everything but popular novels of the kind often checked out of the circulating libraries. Strange, when Charles claimed to be as bookish as herself. Where did he keep his books?

Despite this paucity of interesting reading, there were several volumes of a scientific nature that could always be counted upon for an hour's amusement. Althea selected a large folio book with colored botanical plates and sat down upon a small settee. After half an hour of silent contemplation, the door opened suddenly.

"Cousin!" John came over to the settee. "What have you there?"

Althea showed him the plate she had been studying. "A charming illustration of a pink rose in full bloom."

"Why is it that all females prefer the stodgy rose when the wildflowers are so much more delightful? There is something so easy about flowers in a field—so natural and pure. It calls to mind a rondel I heard once, now let me see—"

"I agree entirely," Althea said, cutting off the proposed rondel. "I was studying the drawing and not the flower. The illustration is quite lifelike and true." She pointed to the center of the flower. "Just look at how the stamen is depicted. I did a number of drawings for my husband's works, so I take every opportunity to improve my craft."

"So you draw, then?"

"Yes, but not quite so well as this. Or at least, not with the same delicacy. It is hard to give a delicate touch to certain subjects—a beetle, for example."

"A beetle?" John wrinkled his nose distastefully.

"Beetles. Quite a number of them. My husband was very fond of beetles. He even discovered one. *Dermestes trentatus*. A very strange sort of animal that feeds on decaying flesh."

Lord John raised his eyebrows. "Sounds like an odd fish, your husband. But this is most pleasing that you draw, for I have in mind a set of illustrations to accompany my poem about the wolf men. And you are the very person to know just how to go about it."

Althea had a sudden inspiration. She closed the book firmly. "Yes, but I lack practice and must surely improve my technique if I am to create drawings that truly capture the terror and pathos of such a subject." She looked at him forlornly. "There is a lack of natural subjects here in town. If I were back at Dettamoor Park, I would not want for subjects, but here," she shrugged her shoulders, "I find so little real beauty in urban life. If there were but a park or a—"

"The park! Why, of course, Cousin Althea, I have been stupid not to think of it before. I have not driven you to promenade in Hyde Park yet. And you must come. Once we have nodded to all the biddies, I can take you around on foot and we shall hit upon the very subjects you require. Is that not a capital idea?"

Althea smiled. "Capital."

So at a few minutes past five o'clock, Althea was assisted up into a phaeton of alarming height. John had, in a fit of dramatic inspiration, had it painted midnight black with blood-red trim. The horses harnessed in front with jet-black traces and silver findings were a well-matched pair of grays. Lord John assured Althea that they were prime goers. As he spread a rug across her knees, he added, "My friend, Finley, wanted to buy them off me, too. Double the price I paid. But one does not meet with such blood and bone every day!"

"No indeed. You did right to keep them. They make such a statement with the black carriage. Like shadow horses leading Charon's chariot down into the underworld."

Lord John seemed much struck. "By Jove, I'd never thought of it in that way. Although it would be better if it were a boat."

Althea repressed a smile. "Not very practical on land."

"True. Still, it's a good image. I have half a mind to use it."

"I'm sure there must be some legend your friend picked up on his travels of a death carriage gliding over the hills with silent horses."

"Bound to be. He told me the people there are fearful strange."

"They must be if they turn into wolves."

John nodded, but it was clear that his thoughts were off on their own flight of fancy.

Althea determined not to bother him because his trancelike state did not seem to impair his ability to handle what turned out to be a very active pair of horses. Althea watched them twitch and pull at their traces whenever they were forced to stand for more than a second, which was often, given the terrible traffic of London. Once, a burly man with an overturned apple cart almost set them to bolt when he leaped into the road to try to retrieve some of his merchandise. And a stiff-looking man with a small dog made them lunge when he brought his carriage too close and the dog began to yap excitedly. Still, Cousin John remained unperturbed and led his equipage safely into the confines of Hyde Park.

"We shall have to go around," John said, leading the carriage into the mass of other vehicles, "and do the pretty first."

Althea craned her neck to perceive which vehicle might contain a repentant Norwich, but there were too many. And in any case, she did not know what sort of carriage he would arrive in. Just as well, since he had suggested the meeting place and must look out for her, not the other way around. She straightened her spine and unfurled a small parasol on a long stick.

John glanced over. "That's a fetching hat, cousin."

"Thank you." Althea reached up and touched the ribbons of her new wide-brim bonnet to make sure they were still tied tightly under one ear. It was an indulgence since she already felt well provisioned, but the green of the dyed straw set her hair off admirably, and the bunch of artificial cherries set rakishly at an angle on the right side was just frivolous enough to tempt a lady so recently used to black felt and inky tulle.

"Although I do not normally follow the fashions of the fairer sex, I do declare that the garments you have lately purchased are vastly more attractive than those raven dresses in which you arrived to London."

"You surprise me, cousin. I understand your abhorrence of the mourning rites; however, given your gothic interests, I would have thought black would have been the preferred color."

"The color, yes, but the form, dear cousin, the form! Why, even burlap cloth may be made acceptable if properly made up. One must approach objects aesthetically—for without proper form, any object may be rendered hideous."

"Even precious gems or gold?"

"Of course! Even those frippery diamonds my mother had the good sense to have stolen. Tell me, Cousin Althea, had you ever seen such a monstrosity?"

Althea looked at him in surprise. "I would not have thought to view the theft of an heirloom in such a light. Although your perspective certainly reduces the disappointment attendant on such a sad event."

"Good riddance, I say. The Levanwoods are far better off with a bank draft from Lloyds than a piece of jewelry that's only real value is as a shocking misuse of trumpery stones."

"Do you consider diamonds to be ugly?"

"All faceted stones fill me with abhorrence. They are too bright and artificial."

"And what, pray tell, are we ladies to wear?"

"Natural materials. Agate or coral. And pearls are in quite a different category, particularly if they are simply strung. When I was in Italy, I bought a very fine necklace—"

He cut off suddenly and turned away.

Althea followed his gaze. Norwich had pulled up in a low-slung carriage that was drawn by a pair of sinewy brown horses whose proud mien bespoke their cost.

John hailed him, "I say, Norwich, those are the finest horses I have ever laid eyes on! Where did you get them?"

"Malverson," Norwich replied, and, turning his head to encompass Althea, he said, "Bingham, Lady Trent, it is a fine day for a drive, is it not?"

John bowed quickly in return, but he was clearly still taken with the horses. "Malverson? But that's impossible! He had those bays, but I've never in my life seen him with such fine animals."

"They were lately acquired, but I suppose he found he could not handle them as he ought."

"The devil, I wish I would have known!"

"My brother informed me of their existence. If you have a mind to purchase something, I shall let him know. I'm sure he knows of a seller who may accommodate you."

"So Verlyn's back again, is he? Where has he come from this time?"

Norwich turned again to Althea. "My brother, Lord George Verlyn, is quite enamored of travel. He is lately returned from the East."

"How interesting, although the present difficulties with Bonaparte must make travel more inconvenient," she replied.

"Yes, but he does not appear to mind it." Norwich tipped his high-crowned hat. "I will not detain you. Bingham, Lady Trent." Then he hesitated a moment. "Lady Trent, I should hope you may be in tomorrow. Good day." And with that, he urged his horses forward.

"Odd duck," John remarked once Norwich was out of earshot.

"He seems not to care much for how others may perceive him."

"No reason why he should. The man's a Croesus. Could buy off anyone he chose, I dare say. Bet Malverson got a pretty penny for those fine horses." John sighed and then shook his head. "Still, it's a good thing for you that he seems to have taken a liking to you. Norwich is exceptionally good ton."

"For a man as partial as you suggest, he has an odd way of seeking my favor. But I suppose my country upbringing is at fault in thinking that general civility is required in such a circumstance."

"Civility? So you are not partial to him?"

"I hardly know the man," she said sharply.

John grinned. "Oh ho, Charles will be sadly put out when he hears that. He thinks your refusal of him is merely a result of Norwich making up to you."

Althea pulled her back straight. "Are my affairs so commonly discussed in the Levanwood household? I had thought at least that matters of the heart must, by their very nature, remain private."

"Not Charles's affairs, certainly. Mama has been on the hunt for a wife for him lo these many years. Prosy fellow, Charles, hard for some ladies to stomach. Can't tell you how many arrangements have fallen through. In any case, Mama is most desirous to see him safely wed. And when you arrived, why, it was plain as a pikestaff that Charles meant to make a go of it. I say, it is good for you that you did turn him down. Serves the fellow right. Been lording about the house like he was king of the world."

"Well!"

"Now don't get your feathers ruffled, cousin. Wouldn't be mentioning it to you if I thought you were one of those squeamish females who took offense at everything."

Althea bit back a retort. Then, recollecting that Cousin John's strange ways and loose tongue just might be useful at some point in the future, she said, "No indeed, I am not. It is just very odd for a female in my circumstances to be suddenly beset by suitors, either purported or real."

"It was not so in Somerset?"

Althea thought of Squire Pettigrew and shuddered. "Jane and I lived quite retired. Do let us leave this subject for one that must be more interesting to your lordship. Where do you propose that we begin our botanical study?"

After several nods and bows to acquaintances in other carriages, John directed the carriage toward a walking path down by the Serpentine and handed the reins to the tiger with strict instructions to keep the horses well exercised in his absence. Then he helped Althea down and offered her his arm.

They passed the next hour quite amicably, discussing the beauty of various plant specimens as Althea sketched them quickly with her charcoal. Althea also drew John out about his love of travel. He had spent several years on the Grand Tour, with most of that time devoted to Italy. He was quite knowledgeable about the language, people, and customs, even going so far as to describe in detail the various delights Rome had to offer. Althea wondered if his return to England had more to do with a lack of continued financing than an inclination for English society.

At the end of this pleasant interlude, John took her for another turn around the park, and she greeted a great many people, only some of whom she could accurately identify to Jane afterward when the ladies met during their toilette in preparation for supper.

"It has certainly been quite an eventful day," Jane said when Althea had recounted the whole to her. "Now I'm sure you will make some remark about preferring the country to town."

"No indeed, I am quite happy that you dragged me to London. But for that, I would not now be embroiled in a very exciting investigation."

Jane merely shook her head.

The evening was less awkward than it might otherwise have been given Lord Charles's late declaration. Lady Levanwood had the forethought to invite several couples for supper followed by cards and the possibility of dancing should one of the ladies desire to display her musical gifts. The couples ranged in age from the elderly Dowager Duchess of Peckham and her new husband, a considerably younger Mr. Smythe, to Lord and Lady Ravenscrest, Lady Ravenscrest having lately emerged from the schoolroom into a marriage with a man twenty years her senior. In between the December and May couples, Viscount Beaconsfield and his lovely but scatterbrained spouse rounded out the assembly.

Althea found herself seated next to Lord Ravenscrest and soon discovered that, despite his taste in simpering underage females, he was a kindred spirit. A chance word led to a long and detailed conversation on the subject of the new farming methods that Althea had caused to be implemented at Dettamoor Park. Then Lord Ravenscrest did Althea the honor of mentioning Sir Arthur's work with admiration. "Some of the best work done these many years," he said. "His death was a great loss to the Society, Lady Trent. A great loss."

Althea assented. "It was always his wish to elevate the study of the lowly animal, particularly the insect, within the Society. They are so overlooked but of such vital importance."

"Indeed, I am of Sir Arthur Trent's opinion. Much may be gained or lost in a single planting because of them. Would that I were able to understand what attracts or repels them.

Improvements in the methods of land rotation and plowing are nothing without the knowledge Sir Arthur sought."

Althea sighed. "If only I had it in my power to continue his work, but my sex precludes me from the hallowed portals of the Royal Society." And then Althea had a wonderful, delightful, wicked idea. She continued, "However, I have in my possession a great many manuscripts written by my husband but not submitted for publication in the *Philosophical Transactions* due to the delicacy of his health. Do you think the Society would be interested in publishing them posthumously?"

"I should think they would," Ravenscrest replied.

"Then I shall begin the process of transcribing his jumble of notes. I assisted him often with this sort of work and prepared his illustrations."

"Please let me know if I may be of assistance in any way. Although not a member myself, I have known Banks and Aldridge for many years, and Randolph Booth as well, if it comes to that."

"Then I shall count myself fortunate if your lordship would do me the honor of an introduction. I read in the *Times* that Lord Aldridge was to give a public lecture on the subject of his extensive botanical studies in the West Indies next Thursday at Somerset House. Shall you attend?"

He smiled. "Most definitely, now that I know my duty."

Later that evening, when the ladies were making desultory conversation over coffee and the delightful honey cakes, Jane said to Althea in a low voice, "You seem very pleased with yourself. Like the cat with the canary."

"Dear Jane, I have finally figured out how to resolve my problem."

"What problem?"

"How to continue my scientific work. Because it would be a shame if all of Arthur's instruction were for naught."

"Arthur's instruction, indeed. As if my brother ever wrote anything half so important before he met you. I am not simple enough to believe that he did everything on his own."

"Thank you for the compliment, but as you know, females are not welcome in the hallowed halls of scholarship. Unless, of course, their roles are properly explained," Althea said.

"As?"

"As a poor widow whose only desire is to publish her deceased husband's work."

"You wouldn't—"

"And why not? Arthur can't mind. In fact, I'm sure he thinks it rather amusing, looking down on us from the heavens."

Jane smiled. "Well, he did like a good joke. And he certainly wouldn't mind being more brilliant in death than he was in life. But wouldn't someone eventually find out?"

"How?"

"At seven and twenty you may have many monographs yet to write."

"I'll deal with that when I have to. Now, I just need to hit upon a topic that would produce a good monograph."

"Beetles?" Jane said.

"That was Arthur's wish, but he had already described his beetle in detail, so any further work would be derivative."

"Isn't that what the Society expects?"

"Yes, but I have never done what others expect. I want a novel idea." Althea hushed quickly as Lady Beaconsfield approached.

"Oh dear, I seem to have set my reticule down and misplaced it." Lady Beaconsfield darted her head this way and that. "Don't let me interrupt your conversation. Ah, there it is." She indicated a table at Althea's elbow. Althea handed it to her.

"Thank you." She sat down in the chair next to Althea. "All this business with the women is so tedious, is it not? Why, one tires so quickly of the usual topics of conversation. The men have the better part, I am sure of it. But then, what can one expect with such superior intellect?"

Althea repressed a smile. "Indeed, you must be right."

CHAPTER EIGHT

The next morning, Althea was ensconced in the library, trying desperately to hit upon a subject for her monograph, when a servant presented her another white envelope on a silver platter. Althea stared at the seal. It must be the three graces. The note from Norwich read as follows:

> *Forgive the manner of communication, madam. I had thought to pay a proper call, but events out of my control have prevented me from waiting upon you. Therefore, I will take the liberty of requesting that you drive with me this afternoon. Assuming your assent, I shall present myself at five o'clock. Should this time not be acceptable, please send word by the same messenger.*
>
> *N.*

"The presumption of the man knows no bounds," Althea muttered to herself. And yet she could find no fault with the plan. The Levanwood party was engaged to dine with the Osterleighs in the evening, but no specific plans had been made for other activities. Unless one counted resting up for supper as an activity worthy of note.

So at five o'clock, Althea found herself waiting patiently in the blue salon while attempting to pretend interest in some needlepoint Jane had thrust upon her to work. Jane herself was equally occupied in what purported to be a fire screen. The servant rapped softly and then pushed the heavy doors apart. "The Duke of Norwich has arrived and asked to speak with your ladyship. I have shown him into the library."

"Ah, yes." Althea stood and shook out the skirts of a new blue velvet gown, which was severely cut and had gold braid at the shoulders and down the bodice. "At least the man is punctual," she added to Jane. And then to the servant in a louder voice, "Please inform him that I will be with him shortly. Thank you."

After retrieving her bonnet and shawl, Althea passed through the door of the library.

Norwich looked over from where he stood, examining one of the walls of books. "Thank you for not making me wait."

"I wouldn't dream of it. Has Your Grace found anything of interest on those shelves?"

He smiled ruefully. "No. I take it that the Levanwoods are not overly fond of reading?"

"Excepting Lord Charles, I don't believe that the present generation has much interest."

He held out his arm. "Come. We have matters to discuss."

"If you like, we might speak here. I am no green girl, so we do not have to conserve the strictest propriety."

"No, much better to get it over with."

Althea opened her mouth to ask what he meant by such a remark, but he'd already taken her arm and guided her to the door.

They didn't speak again until she was tucked up in his phaeton, which was fine but not nearly as spectacular as John's death carriage. The silky brown horses fidgeted and danced until he took them with a firm hand and led them out of the square. Then he said, "Are you comfortable?"

Althea glanced back at the tiger perched behind them in his fine ducal livery and said in a low voice, "Yes, thank you. I suppose I should make some innocuous remarks at this point, but I have not the delicacy of mind for such formalities. I must assume from Your Grace's behavior that you are now reconciled to my interaction with Bow Street?"

He nodded.

"And that Your Grace has determined to assist me in this endeavor."

"You will assist me. And please stop the 'Your Grace' this or that. You may call me Norwich or even Robert if you feel the need, given the roles we have been forced to play. Formality is ridiculous in such a situation."

"And to what roles do you refer? I am at a loss to understand your meaning."

He looked at her in some astonishment. "Surely it is plain to a lady of your intellect?" And when she continued to stare at him, "Why, that of a suitor for your hand, madam. Otherwise, how are we to be seen in each other's company without arousing suspicion?"

"My hand?"

"This cannot come as a surprise. The rumors have run rampant since I had the honor of dancing with you at the Levanwood ball. In fact, I would imagine that some of them have been assiduously spread about by the Levanwoods themselves."

Althea's cheeks flushed pink. "They most assuredly have not!"

He gave her a warning look and replied in a low voice, "Be that as it may, my purpose in entering upon this subject was to explain that, although it may appear to the uninformed that I am pursuing you, you will understand that this is merely a contrivance to catch the Richmond Thief and not—"

"I apprehend exactly what you mean, and I will take this opportunity to explain to you that this speech is entirely unnecessary in light of the fact that our few meetings have shown me exactly how little we would suit. You may have no fears upon that head!"

"I meant no offense, madam."

As they were just in the thick of the carriages on Rotten Row and Althea felt many pairs of eyes upon her, she quelled her anger and gave him her most disarming smile. "Lady Trent will do, or just Althea, if you feel your role calls for it." And then through the clenched teeth of another smile, "As it is, you may do me the favor of explaining exactly in what way I can be of service to you in your pursuit of the Richmond Thief? Clearly, neither one of us was made for inconsequential conversation."

"As you wish. I will be holding a ball in a fortnight. The invitations should have already been sent. Please speak to Lady Levanwood if she has not mentioned this to you. You will attend this function wearing a pair of striking emerald earrings that were a gift from your late husband—"

"Sir Arthur never gave me emeralds."

"Be that as it may, you will wear a pair of emerald earrings and a matching bracelet to the ball. I will supply them, but it will be up to you to circulate the false story of your husband's priceless gifts to you."

"My husband once told me of a plant growing wild in the East Indies that is shaped like a cup with sweet nectar at the bottom. All manner of insects are attracted by the delectable fragrance, but once they approach the pool of ambrosia, they are trapped by the sticky syrup and slowly devoured by the plant for food."

"A plant that devours insects? That cannot be true."

Althea bristled at his tone. "The truth or fiction of the tale is immaterial. The point is that I am the plant and our Richmond Thief is the unfortunate insect. Have I got that right?"

"Precisely right," he replied with asperity.

"I see several problems with the plan."

"I shall make sure you are watched at all times, so no harm may come to you."

"I am not concerned with my safety. I am concerned, however, that the Richmond Thief is not likely to steal jewels while a lady is wearing them. Further, should we fail in our object, I would hate to have you lose such fine gems."

"They have been specially made of paste stones backed with foil, but so finely done that one would have to remove them from the setting to know. And the thief has not always resorted to rank burglary. There have been several cases of ladies who suddenly find a ring or a bracelet unaccountably missing."

"So the thief is both burglar and pickpocket?"

"Apparently."

"And Bow Street is sure that it has accurately attributed these thefts to the thief?"

"All share certain characteristics. First, the thief targets members of the ton exclusively."

"The ton has the most jewelry to steal," Althea replied.

Norwich seemed vaguely annoyed. "Second, the jewels stolen are the family heirloom type."

"Again, those tend to be the most valuable. Else why would they be passed on generation after generation?"

"And third," he said with emphasis, "the thefts always take place in and around a ball or other social function."

"That at least does give rise to certain inferences."

"Such as?"

"The thief must be inconspicuous enough to be able to move in and out of social situations. Someone who may mix in society without causing a disruption. Either a servant or an attendee at these functions."

He sighed. "At least we are finally in agreement."

Althea looked at him with a militant sparkle in her eye. "Do we disagree that often, sir? This is not a propitious start to our pretend courtship."

"If I may speak plainly—"

"Don't tell me that your past speeches are a product of restraint?"

"Lord, woman, do give me a chance to speak! I have never met such an exasperating female in my life."

Althea drew herself up. "And I have never met a man who felt so free to tell another person that she is without brains or utility. Really sir, you have gone out of your way to insult me, and as much as I wish to be of use to Bow Street, I am beginning to think that I would be better off to pursue the investigation myself. At least then I could be more than a dumb lure and would not be subject to the tyranny of one who clearly holds me in low regard."

A carriage of ladies Althea didn't know passed by at that moment and they stared at her. Norwich gave them a curt nod and they obediently moved on. When they had passed, he said in a low voice, "Please remember where you are."

"This is ridiculous. Take me home at once!"

He looked at Althea with a strange expression. Perhaps shock, perhaps anger, perhaps some emotion she couldn't name. "No, madam," he said more quietly. "Let me begin again."

"Why should I let you?"

That was clearly not the response he had expected. "Because—" Then he pulled the carriage up short and called back to the tiger, "Take the reins, Hutchins. I wish to walk with Lady Trent."

Norwich jumped down nimbly and held his hand out to Althea. "Please, madam." His voice was softer now, almost pleading.

Althea hesitated. Although the walking path was in plain view of the other occupants of the park, Norwich's change of behavior unnerved her. "You may call me Lady Trent," she said to say something.

"Althea."

She relented and held out her hand. He took it, assisted her in dismounting, and then tucked her hand in his arm. They began to stroll down the walking path among the clumps of dashing young men and blushing ladies. It felt strangely familiar to walk with him.

This is just how I used to walk with Arthur, she thought, and then she pushed the thought away. Norwich was nothing like Arthur.

Once they were out of earshot of the other pedestrians, he said, "I suppose this is the moment I should offer a profuse apology."

She looked up at him just as the sunlight caught his golden hair, creating a glittering halo around his head. He seemed otherworldly in that moment, like a gilded angel from one of those moldering psalters still safely stored on the shelves of the library at Dettamoor Park. And the thought of this golden man walking beside her with her hand tucked neatly in his arm made her feel strangely lightheaded. She clutched desperately at her former composure. "Given our prior acquaintance, I feel sure that such an apology will not be forthcoming."

Instead of the thundering anger she had been expecting, Norwich began to laugh. A slow rumble at first, then swelling to a full-throated laugh that echoed around them.

Althea's shoulders relaxed. "I did mean that seriously."

Norwich pulled himself back together and wiped his streaming eyes. "I know you did. Lady Trent, what a strange pair we make. Come, let's take a turn and discuss what we are to do."

"No more tyrannical dictates?"

"I have entirely given up trying to guide you."

She smiled archly. "You are a quick learner, my lord. Sir Arthur took several years before he reached the same conclusion."

"Your husband was a saint."

"So I have been told."

CHAPTER NINE

After that stroll in Hyde Park, Norwich became a fixture at the house, much to Charles's evident frustration. But he wasn't the only male to make his presence known in Grosvenor Square. Sir Neville had taken to paying social calls several weeks back, inviting the ladies, including Lady Levanwood, to such sedate diversions as would find favor with refined town-bred women. And upon learning that Althea and Jane were determined to attend Aldridge's lecture, he offered his services as escort. In this, he was thwarted somewhat by Charles's expressing a desire to accompany the ladies himself.

That morning Althea awoke with a splitting headache. As she was not normally prone to such maladies, she examined her activity on the previous day for any clues, but nothing stood out. After a turn in Hyde Park with John, she had returned home, and then in the evening they had attended a musical performance at the house of Baroness Kamynski, one of the flighty, overdressed women who seemed to make up Lady Levanwood's circle. Granted, she had drunk some wine with supper, but nothing so as to produce deleterious effects. And she had virtuously refused anything stronger than coffee afterward. Charles had even remarked favorably on her cool-headed abstinence when he tried to offer her a claret cup.

So her precise raven recordings skipped a day as she lay in bed, trying to recover her strength in time for the lecture. Fortunately, the combination of a darkened room and toast dipped in weak tea worked its magic, and by the afternoon she was dressed and ready for enlightenment.

The odd quartet departed Grosvenor Square for the Strand. Althea felt her heart beat a little faster at the thought of entering the grand portal of Somerset House. Arthur had experienced his greatest triumph there—a lecture on the discovery of the beetle that ultimately bore his name. And Althea had asked him to repeat the details of his speech so many times that she felt a strange sense of déjà vu as she entered the expansive patio and climbed the stairs to the rooms occupied by the Royal Society.

The crowd gathered in the close anteroom was a mix of luminaries and the interested parties whose abundant patronage had done so much to foment the progress of science in the new century. Althea saw Lord Ravenscrest standing across the room by the elegant chimneypiece and caught his eye. He hurried over.

"Lady Trent, how delightful to see you again," he said. "I have mentioned your manuscripts to Aldridge, and he was very excited by the prospect of continuing Sir Arthur's work from beyond the grave. We shall speak to him after the lecture. Ah, Carlton, good to see you again, and Miss Trent, delighted. And Sir Neville Tabard, I don't believe I've ever seen you at one of the Society lectures before."

"'Tis the present exulted company," Sir Neville said gallantly. "It is a great stimulation to the intellect."

"Indeed," Ravenscrest replied with an admirable lack of sarcasm. "Come, ladies and gentlemen, I believe it is now time to be seated."

He guided them into the square meeting room, which had carved moldings and large fireplace. The light from the broad windows cast a honey glow over the proceedings and made Althea reflect that this was just what she could hope heaven might be—beauty and science joined together in perfect union. Ravenscrest selected chairs three rows back from the velvet-draped podium and then sat down next to Althea, forcing Charles to wedge himself in between Jane and Sir Neville, whose corset creaked ominously as he sat down.

"Why, I never thought these scientific lectures could be such a tight squeeze," Sir Neville said. "There are ever so many people. It quite takes my breath away."

Althea heard Charles mumble something, but she couldn't make out all of the words. She bit her lip to keep from smiling. She would have been lying to say that Charles's discomfiture did not amuse her greatly. She could have had more sympathy if he were not forever following her about the house with a pained look upon his face. It was as if he meant to work upon feelings of guilt in order to achieve her assent, and that simple-minded tactic galled her. Althea was not a sentimental heroine from a lending-library novel, for goodness sake!

At least she could turn her mind to intellectual pursuits for the hour of the lecture. As it turned out, Aldridge's speech was interesting on a number of levels. There was the knowledge Aldridge sought to impart, the reaction of the crowd, and a low conversation on various scientific subjects with Lord Ravenscrest at her side. To add to these attractions, there was also the entertainment of watching her own party.

Sir Neville feigned attention for a good quarter of an hour before his eyelids began to droop dangerously. Charles's interest lasted longer, but then he fell into contemplation of the intricate plaster ceiling, with its famous medallions of the late King Charles and the present King George. When he thought she wouldn't notice, he studied Althea with that look of an abused canine upon his face. Jane studied the bonnet of a woman in front of them. Admittedly, it was incredibly ugly.

After the lecture ended and the captive audience was released, Ravenscrest fulfilled his promise and took Althea to meet Lord Aldridge. Aldridge not only seemed pleased to make the acquaintance, but also caused Lord Banks to join their small party. That luminary said, "Lady Trent, Aldridge has told me that Sir Arthur was actively working before his death and that you might have some manuscripts of interest to the Society."

"Indeed, my lord. And it was his fondest wish that I might somehow seek publication for them after his death."

"Quite a determined man, your husband. I don't see why we couldn't entertain the notion, provided they are of the caliber of his other work."

"I feel sure that they are. The only problem at this point is one of making a presentable copy for the Society's review.

His notes are in a jumble, I'm afraid, and may take some time to sort out. If I could submit a finished manuscript in the next several months, would that give the Society ample time for review?"

Banks turned to Aldridge. "I should think so, don't you?"

Aldridge nodded. "Certainly."

A third gentleman approached the group. "What is this I hear of posthumous manuscripts?" He was a grizzled man with sharp gray eyes.

"Why Lord Ephraim, you remember Sir Arthur Trent, don't you?"

"Humph, of course I do. Little beetles and frogs and so forth."

"Yes." Aldridge smiled apologetically at Althea. "This is Lady Trent, and she says she has manuscripts Trent meant to publish. I think the Society must be interested.

Randolph Booth gave Althea a hard stare. "How do you do. Seems too big a task for such a small lady."

Althea felt a stab of anxiety that quickly flared into anger. Lord Ephraim Randolph Booth was not going to stop her. She pasted a bright smile on her face. "I assure you, Lord Ephraim, that I am perhaps the only person in the world who would do my husband's work justice."

"Beg your pardon, but that is hardly likely. The female mind is not calibrated for the grueling task of preparing scientific manuscripts. Your ladyship would be better to have Aldridge or Banks here assemble Sir Arthur's papers."

"Of course, Lady Trent, I would only be too happy—" Aldridge said.

Althea could feel her chance slipping away. She drew herself up and replied with as much affability as she could muster. "Were that I could simply hand my husband's notes to one of you learned gentlemen. Alas, Sir Arthur was not at all careful in the composition of his papers, so they display a deplorable lack of penmanship. They would be quite unintelligible to anyone not familiar with his scrawling alphabet. Indeed, it is only the years of experience as his wife that have allowed me to decipher any portion of his correspondence."

"Oh, I see." Aldridge turned to Randolph Booth. "Then I think we must let her try to put them in order. It would be a great loss to the Society to reject a member's study all for the lack of a legible hand."

Randolph Booth did not look pleased. "Do as you see fit, Aldridge, but I can only hope that the new manuscripts are of the caliber fit for the *Philosophical Transactions*."

Althea left Somerset House as if floating above the clouds. No matter the subterfuge, no matter the very evident doubt upon Lord Ephraim's face, no matter that she did not yet have a topic for her manuscript, Althea had finally found a way to achieve her heart's desire. If only her father were still alive to share her triumph. Although Arthur supported her ambitions and Jane was her confidant, her father was the only one who had ever understood how much Althea wanted for herself. Her work and her triumph. For now she would work within the Society's strictures, but one day they would come to know.

That evening, as Althea was preparing for a ball to be held at the Earl of Cumberland's house, Jane walked in from her adjoining room. "What a fuss! I swear we never had the problems at Dettamoor Park that they have here.

The servant quarters are in an uproar again. Buxton will not be up to attend to you this evening."

"What is all the fuss about?"

"Seems Mr. Langley, the marquess's valet, has disappeared. Apparently disappearances are quite a common occurrence in this household."

"Disappeared?"

"Vanished. Run off or something. He wasn't here in the morning."

"Remind me again: he was that short, thin fellow with the face like a rat and those giant side-whiskers?"

"Yes. According to Sally, he wasn't much liked by anyone but the marquess."

"But then how is Mrs. Buxton involved?"

"Well," Jane threw herself into a chair, "apparently she is indisposed after dealing with that servant girl Mary, who was in high hysterics again this morning."

"Why was Mary in hysterics?"

"Mary claims Langley isn't missing, but rather dead. Or was dead early this morning when she went down to the garden."

Althea came from her dressing table and took the chair facing Jane. "So is Langley dead or missing?" If only that headache hadn't kept Althea from her morning bird ritual. Then again, maybe John had been awake at that hour and might have seen what happened. Or was even involved. Althea shuddered.

"No one knows, for when Mary brought one of the maids, a girl named Bridgett, out to see the body, it had disappeared."

"Vanished?"

"That is the story Sally got from Bridgett. She's the one who'll be up to help with your toilette in a minute or two. Seems she was training under Mrs. Buxton."

"But this is too peculiar for words. Has Bow Street been sent for?"

"Bridgett didn't say, but I can't imagine that they have. The story seems too fanciful to be true."

"And yet a girl like Mary wouldn't risk her position with a lie such as this. There must be some explanation."

There was a rap at the door. Jane stood up. "That will be Bridgett. Send her to me when you are finished, for I have silk flowers that will just go with this gown, and I want her to place them in my hair."

"Flowers in your hair? My, what special care you have taken of late."

"I'll have none of your commentary." Jane slipped through the door before Althea could reply.

Despite gentle persuasion, Althea could not cull more information from the skittish Bridgett than Jane had already imparted to her, except that Bridgett said that Mary talked of the body lying near the back gate. Althea set off for the ball resolved to hunt Mary down the next morning and wring the rest of the details of the story from her.

Once the Levanwood party had negotiated their hosts' receiving line, Charles claimed Althea for the dance that was just forming.

"We have had little opportunity for conversation, cousin," he said.

Althea assented without much enthusiasm. They came to the line of dancers and stood opposite. "And do you have a particular topic of conversation you desire to pursue?"

Charles gave her a warm look. "You know the topic closest to my heart."

Althea adjusted her face into what she hoped was a pious look. "And you know my sentiments on that topic. Although I have put on colors, my heart has not."

The music started, and Charles approached her in the steps of the dance. When he was at her elbow, he said in a low voice, "Strange then that you should so encourage other men. Perhaps your heart is not as broken as you claim."

Althea did a slow turn around him and replied, "*Encourage* is a strange word. I would say *humor* is a better one. Who would willingly cross a duke?"

They went down the line and then came back together. "So it is your desire not to offend that impels you to drive with Norwich in Hyde Park at every opportunity?"

"I accept such invitations as are extended to me."

"I have been remiss in my invitations?"

Althea met his gaze squarely. "No sir, you have been a gentleman in not seeking to press me too hard."

He leaned in ever so slightly, a strange, hard glitter in his eyes. "I wish I were a rake."

The dance separated them again, and when they came back together, Althea abruptly changed the conversation.

Unfortunately, Norwich arrived soon thereafter to engage her for a country dance.

"We mustn't be seen together quite so frequently," Althea remarked to him as he took her hand.

"Why is that? We have gotten on famously since I capitulated to your demands."

She looked at him archly. "My demands? I have capitulated in all important respects to yours." And then, before he could argue, "But no, it is because such close collaboration has given rise to the most unwanted speculation."

The music started, and he said, "That was the idea, if you remember."

"I remember. However, I cannot be seen to favor you when others have an equal claim to my company."

Norwich gave her a sharp look. "You have promised—no, insisted—on helping Bow Street. You cannot decline now just because you have developed a tendre for someone else."

"My lord, you mistake the matter. I have indicated to all concerned that I am not yet ready to enter into a romantic attachment. My bereavement is of too recent a date."

"Is that true?"

It was Althea's turn for a sharp look. "That is a very rude question."

Norwich was taken aback, but then he recovered. A slow smile spread across his face. "I don't believe anyone has ever had the temerity to say that to me before."

"They should have."

"Undoubtedly," he replied gamely. "But rest assured, Lady Trent, when the Richmond Thief is safely caught, we may be seen to argue as much as you like. I will even put about the story that you refused me because of your continuing attachment to your late husband."

"It is certainly a better story than that you got tired of me."

"I was thinking of the always acceptable *we did not suit*."

Althea smiled. "At least that has a ring of truth about it."

"Yes," was all he replied.

When the dance ended, other gentlemen sought Althea out, and she went from one partner to another until she ended with Cousin John, who chattered on as usual about the progress of his wolf man sonnet.

Althea casually inserted a question about the missing valet, but John disclaimed all knowledge. "You can't tell what mischief servants will be up to. That fellow Langley never could select clothes. Don't know what father was doing with him all these years. Maybe now he'll leave off those ghastly brocade waistcoats."

At the end of the country dance, John was just about to walk Althea back to where Jane sat ensconced next to Sir Neville on a bench when a gentleman passed them by and John said, "Verlyn! Just the man I was looking for."

The gentleman turned, and Althea easily saw the resemblance to his elder brother. Except that Verlyn was darker and handsomer than his brother. There was also a certain air of lurking mischief in Lord George Verlyn's brown eyes that drew Althea in.

"Bingham," he said. "Good to see you again."

"And you. I say, how did you happen to find out about those fine horses of Malverson's? It puts me all out of patience, keeping a pair like that out of reach of the rest of us."

"Just the right information at the right moment, my dear fellow." He looked at Althea expectantly.

"Let me introduce my cousin, Lady Trent. Lady Trent, Lord George Verlyn."

He bowed. "Ah, Lady Trent. I have heard much of your beauty and intelligence."

She curtsied. "Be on your guard, sir, for false rumors."

Verlyn laughed. "You do not disappoint, Lady Trent, I assure you." And then because the musicians were just tuning up for another dance, he extended his hand. "Would you do me the honor, or does another gentleman have a prior claim?"

Althea put her hand in his. "No sir, I am not otherwise engaged."

As they walked to their positions, she said, "How do you find London, Lord George? I had heard that you have lately returned from extensive foreign travel."

"Not much changed. Like any of the other great cities, its fundamentals do not alter. I understand from those false rumors that you are lately come from Somerset."

"Yes, this is my first season in London."

"Let us hope it will not be the last." They executed the first turn.

"That depends on many circumstances."

"Such as?" The dance separated them, and Althea took the arm of another gentleman.

When Verlyn finally came back to her, she said, "My son's scholarly progress—he is presently boarding with his tutor in preparation for Eton—and my ability to prepare my husband's manuscripts for publication with the Royal Society."

"Not the usual answers of a gentlewoman, but then, you appear to be somewhat out of the common way."

"I'm not sure how to take that, sir."

Verlyn replied, "In the most complimentary way possible, I hope. But what of yourself, madam? Are there no delights that will bring you to London for your own sake?"

She was back to another partner and waited until Verlyn returned. "Many, but I am a sad bluestocking and enjoy best the solitary pleasures of contemplation and reading. Those may be had aplenty in Somerset."

"Dettamoor Park must have quite a library, then."

She looked him in the eye. "You have done your research if you know the name of a small estate in Somerset."

He met her gaze with one of those mischievous looks. "Only when it is home to a heretofore unknown lady now hailed as the toast of London."

Althea did not have a ready reply, so she said nothing as the dance parted them once more. When Verlyn rejoined her, he looked at her expectantly.

"Dettamoor Park does have quite a library," Althea said calmly. "My husband's ancestors were avid scholars, and I have had the benefit of their investment."

"Austell Abbey is much the same, and my brother had quite a large number of volumes transported to London. Like you, madam, he can always be found with his nose in a book."

"So he mentioned to me once."

Verlyn chuckled. "What a paltry fellow! Instead of well-executed compliments, my poor brother prattles on about books? How disappointing. One expects more from an older and wiser sibling."

"The fault is mine, I fear. I asked the question."

Verlyn would have none of it, and when the dance joined them once more he added, "My duty is now clear. I pledge to do everything within my power to prove to you that our family is not the dull set of persons you have been led to expect."

Something in the sinuous inflection of his voice made a shiver of delight run up Althea's spine.

CHAPTER TEN

The next morning, after barely three hours of sleep, Althea awoke just before the first light of dawn. It was a struggle to wrestle her sluggish body out of bed, but she had to get down to the yard and search for clues to Mary's fantastic story. As every dress she owned required assistance, she pulled a thick wrapper around her shift, lit the small beeswax taper at her bedside, and hoped she could slip out of the house without being seen. She had a near miss with a scullery maid carrying a bucket of hot water from the kitchen, but otherwise the late return of the guests from the Cumberland ball favored her unseen progress through the darkened house.

She let out her breath when she reached the garden. Even an eccentric provincial widow knew that wandering around outside her bedchamber in a wrapper and shift was highly irregular. *They will say I am a candidate for Bedlam*, she thought to herself as she made her way slowly around the yard, the candle flickering dangerously in the faint breeze of the night. There was only a quarter moon in the sky, throwing off barely enough light to see one foot in front of the other.

She reached the back gate and then crouched down, guarding the fragile flame with her cupped hand. The ground in front of the gate was packed smooth by common use and so impervious to tracks or other marks of any sort. Althea set the candle down and moved her hands slowly across the ground's surface. It felt vaguely damp, but that could be the dew. She lifted a hand to her nose. Nothing but the smell of dirt.

She spied her raven tucked neatly under the bush and held the candle over the poor shrunken body. The light of one small candle wasn't enough to see the detail she needed for precise measurements. However, the flickering flame did reveal the familiar spiny larvae feeding relentlessly on the bird's desiccated muscle. Those squirmy creatures would not become the speckled beetles she knew so well from Arthur's research for at least another month.

Sir Arthur Trent had planned to do a monograph outlining the life cycle of the *Dermestes trentatus*, but Althea knew that such a monograph would not be sufficient for her own ambitions. If she could only conjure up a more exciting topic. The decay of the raven held interest for her, but as yet her observations had not yielded fundamental truths of any kind. No, she needed something novel and potentially useful to other scientists.

A yawn overtook her, and she sighed, the fatigue of the past several days finally catching up. Her bed had never seemed so enticing. In fact, she was just ready to return to the house when she noticed a short length of rope caught on the bush above the body of her bird. She picked it up. It was a silk cord of some sort, like the kind used for a bellpull, but ripped and frayed at one end. The other end was bound in a tassel. That had not been there the other morning. She picked up the candle and started back to the house, carrying the cord between her fingers.

All of a sudden the gate flew open. Althea ducked back instinctively, nestling her body against the bushes, and quickly snuffed the candle. A figure carrying a lantern emerged from the road. Althea caught enough of the shape in the pale light to tell that it was a man. Probably a servant just returning from some early-morning chore for the great house. But instead of bustling into the house, the man simply set the lantern at his feet and stood, looking up at the sky.

Could it be Cousin John? Althea waited and waited, but the man made no move to leave. Althea felt her strength ebbing as she crouched in the bushes. She looked up. The sky already showed pale streaks of pink. Soon it would be light enough for them to see each other. Althea edged closer to the house, walking silently, slowly, using all her faculties to move like the cat Magistrate Read had called her. She was almost there, almost to the door when she accidentally stepped on a twig. She felt it crack under her foot and winced. She looked over. The man turned. In the half-light of the lantern, she could see his profile. He picked up the lantern and held it in her direction.

"Cousin?" John said.

Althea resolutely stood. "Yes."

"Lovely morning."

"Indeed. I should go back."

"A word of advice, you'll catch cold dressed like that."

Althea instinctively pulled the wrapper close. "You're probably right, but the night was so lovely, and I couldn't sleep."

John nodded. "I had the same thought. The dawn is resplendent in her glorious majesty."

"Goodnight, cousin."

John looked up at the sky and then back at Althea. "Good morning, Althea."

She ran back into the house.

After an hour's sleep, Althea awoke to her usual routine. She partook of a solitary breakfast and then went in search of Mary. But Mary was not to be found anywhere in the house. Althea had taken pains to establish an unusually free and easy discourse with Mr. Mauston over their mutual interest in food, and this relationship gave her access to much of the servants' gossip. She sought him out next, but none of the servants, including the kitchen staff, had told him anything. However, when Althea finally encountered Mrs. Buxton, she found out why.

"She left the Levanwood employ yesterday," Buxton said.

"Yesterday?"

"Yes. We felt it best considering the circumstances. Decorum in a household is very important. The rest of the staff were not informed. After everything, the marchioness felt it was best to keep the dismissal as quiet as possible."

"Do you know where she might have gone?"

"One would assume a register office."

"Yes, very likely. Was she originally placed with the Levanwood family by a particular office?"

"She was hired from Westminster's."

"Thank you."

Althea returned to her room, lost in thought. Norwich was to come for her at five o'clock to drive in the park, but she had no other fixed plan for the day. Perhaps a little shopping with Jane. She rapped gently on Jane's door and then walked in. The room was still dark, so Althea pulled open the drapes, letting the bright light of the morning stream in. She heard soft moaning from the curtained bed, so she pulled the curtains aside and stuck her head in. "Jane, you must come with me."

Jane squinted at her. "Althea? Good heavens, girl, what are you about?"

"No more time for beauty sleep, Jane dear. We must get out to the register offices."

"Register offices? Whatever for?"

"To find Mary. They've turned her off, and we must speak to her. You said you wished to help me."

Jane sighed wearily. "Unfortunately, I did. But what makes you think Mary was telling the truth about what she saw? And what connection could any of that have with the Richmond Thief?"

"No connection I can think of, but any murder should interest Bow Street."

"I have no dependence on the ravings of a hysterical servant girl."

"We will see how hysterical she is when we speak with her."

But that was not to be, for Mary seemed to have vanished into thin air. Or at the very least, she seemed not to be in need of further employment, for neither Westminster's nor any of the other register offices had any word of her.

"That is very strange," Althea said as she climbed up into their carriage. "Perhaps Mary has decided to forgo the register fee and seek employment from the papers."

"Or she registered under a different name. Do we even know that Mary was her name?"

"No, I suppose not, but one would assume the register office would require some documentation in order to place her."

"And Westminster's seems to be the preferred office for the Levanwood household. I heard Bella say that they have a hard time keeping undermaids employed—they always wish to move on to a better position after they are trained," Jane said.

"These London houses must have a terrible time of it. Why, the servants of Dettamoor Park are all known to us from birth."

"Before birth," Jane replied. "Many of their families have worked for the Trent family for several generations."

"Let us hope that they tell better tales of us than what I hear sometimes of others."

"Such as?" Jane said.

"The Levanwoods are a strange family. Some give as much trouble as they are able, and some are barely mentioned. Charles, for instance. I have never heard him so much as spoken of. John, on the other hand, causes all sorts of fuss. Seems he stays out till all hours and must have coffee first thing in the morning, before he even washes up."

"And how did you hear that?"

"A kitchen maid complaining to another just outside the breakfast parlor. Confirmed by a stray comment from

Mauston when I spoke at length with him about the recipe for those honey cakes."

"Be careful what you listen to. One day they may be talking about you."

"They already are. You and I are considered fine ladies, by the way," Althea said.

"Because?"

"We are not forever fancying ourselves ill like Lady Levanwood and requiring tea and biscuits to be brought to our chambers five times a day."

Jane laughed. "You are incorrigible."

"The Levanwood household is nothing so much as an anthill. Like the lowly ants, we all have our roles to play."

"And what is yours?"

"That, my dear Jane, is yet to be determined."

The carriage came to a halt. "Are we in Grosvenor Square?" Jane said.

"No. Harding Howell in Pall Mall."

Jane raised her brows.

"Shopping. Come quick, dear, we must hurry and make some trifling purchases else they will all know what we have been about."

CHAPTER ELEVEN

The night of the Norwich ball, Althea dressed with extra care. A new gown from Madame Longet had just arrived that morning—an ivory confection with point lace and pale green and ivory satin ribbons cunningly formed into a garden of roses across the fitted bodice and down the back of the trailing skirt. Although Althea's status as a widow entitled her to wear some elaborate turban or lace-festooned cap, she had come to realize that such overwrought styles did not suit her and had kept to her usual simplicity, this time in the form of a wide band of the same ribbon flowers placed by Buxton's expert hands on the crown of her head.

The emerald earrings and bracelet made their appearance while Buxton was still affixing the flowers. Althea snapped the case open. If she hadn't known better, she would have thought they were real.

Buxton clearly did. "How lovely, Lady Trent."

"They were a present from Sir Arthur, just before he died," Althea said. In actual fact, Althea had spent more time talking about emeralds than any other subject the last two weeks. She doubted if there was a person in England who did not know that she had emeralds and was to wear them to the Norwich ball.

"Sir Arthur had excellent taste."

"He did." Althea affixed first one earring and then the other. Then she held up her wrist for Buxton to do the clasp on the bracelet. "There. Shall I be a success, Mrs. Buxton, do you think?"

Buxton nodded. "The loveliest lady at the ball for sure."

But Althea wasn't too sure when she saw the striking collection of people coming up the stairs. "I feel grossly underdressed," she whispered to Jane, gesturing ahead of her at a tall, shapely woman in a gown made entirely of silver net.

"Nonsense," Jane replied. "That dress is almost obscene. And she appears to have dampened her petticoats. I never thought to see such sights in England, but I hear that Lamb woman will be here tonight, so we are sure to see another disgraceful show."

Althea pretended to share Jane's indignation but really wondered what it would be like to have such a figure and such confidence. Next to a woman like that, Althea was a poor, drab nothing. A sparrow next to a peacock. Although that comparison wasn't apt given her gender. Still, a small part of her wished nature had given her a more striking carapace. Then she had a delightful idea. She could change her carapace by dressing as an insect for the masquerade ball that Lady Shirling was to give in another month. A butterfly, perhaps, or a delicate-winged moth. She would speak to Madame Longet as soon as possible.

Norwich caught sight of the Levanwood party, and when the receiving line moved enough to place Althea in front of him, he said softly, "Lovely as always, Lady Trent. Sir Arthur's emeralds look charming."

"Enough like ambrosia?" she replied.

"Any insect would find you irresistible."

Jane, who stood close enough to catch Norwich's reply, looked at Althea strangely, but Althea merely smiled and moved on.

The plan was to mingle, show the fabricated emeralds off as much as possible, and then hope for the best. Norwich had assured her that she would be watched at all times, but by whom and how he wouldn't say.

Sir Neville had approached the Trent ladies almost as soon as they crossed the threshold and managed to capture Jane's attention by remarking on the degeneration of morals evident in the dress of the faster society ladies. "Caro Lamb is quite beyond the pale this evening!"

Jane looked eagerly about her and then, spying a woman in a dress that clung to her curves like a second skin, exclaimed, "Aha!"

Althea continued to hover by Lady Levanwood, who immediately sought out Lady Jersey and engaged her in a liberal exchange of ton gossip and a round condemnation of Lady Pickney's latest bon mot. That proved to be only slightly more entertaining than Jane's diatribe against muslin gauze and skin-colored chemises. Fortunately, the musicians began to tune their instruments, and Lord Casterleigh seized the opportunity to ask Althea to dance. Other partners followed, and it was well past midnight when Althea, bracelet and earrings still intact, met up with Norwich.

As he led her out on to the floor she remarked, "I fear I have not made myself tempting enough for the Richmond Thief."

"The night is still young."

"And what am I to do when he comes?"

"Nothing. Do not fight him. Let him take the jewels, and we will do the rest."

Althea looked at Norwich, ready to argue, but then thought better of it. If Norwich meant to have his own way, then it was best to let him think he had it. Althea would make up her mind when the time came.

Norwich seemed to sense her mood of resignation. "Patience, Lady Trent. You will have time enough for adventure when the Richmond Thief is caught."

"And what adventure might that be?"

"One of your own devising, I'm sure. I have heard it said that you have an interest in the Royal Society."

"That is adventure of a very different sort."

"But clearly fruitful. And what, pray tell, was the subject of your husband's scholarship?" Norwich must have made more than casual inquiries.

They took their places.

"Many things, but he was fascinated by insects before he died."

"And are you equally interested?" Norwich said it lightly, as if in jest.

Althea looked at him. "Yes, I am."

"But surely such a subject is repulsive to a delicately bred female?"

"You have a very paltry notion of delicately bred females, sir." And then, because her irritation could not be contained, she proceeded in between turns to describe in detail all of her observations of the insects slowly skeletonizing the raven's corpse, adding at the end, "So you see, there is justice in the animal world such that the predatory raven eventually becomes the prey."

Norwich looked at her dumbly for a moment and replied, "I see."

"You see what, sir?"

"I see that we must find the thief and end this charade as soon as possible."

Althea gritted her teeth, unaccountably stung by his disgust of her work. "The sooner the better."

The song ended, and they parted. Althea was engaged to dance by Major Conrad, a fine-looking gentleman in regimentals who seemed to form part of Charles's particular friends. Then Charles himself appeared to claim a dance and stare dolefully into Althea's eyes. He ended the number by accidentally treading on the train of her gown and tearing it. This put her all out of patience with the men of her species, so she flitted off to the cloakroom before Charles could utter one more anguished apology.

After getting one of the cloakroom attendants to assist her with the needed repairs, Althea flitted out again, still fizzing with righteous indignation. "I am in no mood for company," she told herself, and she decided to walk a bit through the hallways of Norwich House until her temper cooled. And in this roundabout way, she found herself suddenly in front of what must be the library. The light from the hall combined with the flicker of a low flame in the grate illuminated the pale outlines of book-lined walls and a large desk set back underneath a heavily curtained window. As a fly drawn into the delicate tangle of a spider's web, Althea's steps led her inside, across the thick plush of the carpet to the desk. What did Norwich occupy his days with? Clearly not scientific observation. And yet the temptation to see inside his world was too great. She leaned over the desk, examining the papers neatly stacked on the blotter. Letters, but to whom? She couldn't tell in the faint light. She leaned over farther, then heard a sound behind her—the door, shutting fast.

She whirled around, a scream on her lips, but was too late, for the man had a vicelike grip around her waist and a gloved hand over her mouth. She struggled, but he was clearly too strong for her to repel. She stopped struggling to recoup her forces and give her time to think.

"Remain calm, Lady Trent, and no harm shall come to you," he whispered in her ear.

It was a strange whisper, like an actor upon the stage. *He must be concealing his true voice,* she thought.

She nodded and felt the arm about her waist slowly loosen, but he did not let her go. "Now if you promise not to scream, I will remove my hand from your mouth."

She nodded again, calculating just how far she could run if she did decide to scream, but his arm held her tight.

He removed his hand from her mouth, but instead of letting her go, he turned her in his arms so she faced him. He wore a dark mask of some sort, tied tight around his eyes and down his nose, obscuring his features beyond recognition. The smell of a strong, dark cologne she did not recognize hung in the air.

"Are you the Richmond Thief?" she whispered. Despite her initial fear, she had to admit that there was something wickedly romantic about the dark room and the flicker of soft light across his masked face. Almost like one of those dreams that woke her at night, aching and unsatisfied.

"A brilliant deduction, madam."

"If you let me go, I will give you my emeralds straight away."

He laughed softly. "No indeed, I shall not be fobbed off with such paltry pastes."

"Pastes?" she said too loudly.

"Shush or I shall have to take drastic measures."

"No, no. I mean, how did you know?"

There was that low rumble of a laugh again. "Because no emeralds are as perfectly matched as the set you wear. And if it were, it would be owned by a family more prominent than the Trents."

"Logical," Althea replied in grudging admiration. "And so what do we do now? If you let me go, I promise not to mention the matter to anyone."

"You are a lady of your word, but this is your warning. Do not pursue me further or you will live to regret it."

"What will you do to me?"

"Are you afraid?"

Althea had to admit that she did not have the advantage of the situation, so she nodded.

"Good," he paused as if considering and then said, "but I have a far more agreeable object in mind tonight."

She tilted her head up, outwardly defiant. "Such as?"

He ran one gloved finger down her cheek. "I have been watching you, waiting for just the right moment." His eyes bored into hers, as if gauging her reaction. Then, before she could protest, his lips met her lips.

His mouth was soft and persuasive, not forcing her, but rather pulling her in. Althea's initial surprise was quickly replaced by the strangest sensation—her pulse accelerated and a giddy warmth wormed its way down her spine and out through her veins until every inch of her tingled. The sound of her heart pounded in her ears.

This must be what passion feels like. Angina pectoris, she thought as she found herself burrowing farther into the stranger's arms and kissing him back with a reckless abandon completely alien to her. And to think such feelings existed inside drab little Althea Claire. She could have laughed, but instead she let the madness sweep through her, losing all sense of the world around her save for the pleasure of the thief's kiss.

The thief pulled back first, saying with a growling whisper, "You will drive me mad." He let her go suddenly. "Leave now."

"But?" Her head spun dangerously and she stumbled backward.

He caught her. "Steady." He ran his hand slowly down her arm. "Leave, I beg of you, before I do something I will regret." Even in a disguised whisper, Althea could not fail to understand his meaning.

"Oh." A part of her rejoiced at the maintenance of her good reputation, but another part felt suddenly desolate. "Shall I ever see you again?"

"For your sake, I hope not. Now, go." There was a veiled menace in the stage whisper.

Althea regained her bearings in the darkened room and then walked resolutely to the door. She opened it, but when, like a bewildered Orpheus, she turned back, he was gone.

CHAPTER TWELVE

That night Althea tossed in her bed, shaken by strange amorphous dreams. She awoke with a start at dawn, both ashamed of her conduct the night before and filled with a desire to move forward with the investigation. No midnight warning from a masked stranger was going to put her off. She threw open the bed curtains, pulled open the drapes, and rang the bell. A bleary-eyed housemaid appeared several minutes later.

"You rang, milady?"

"Yes. Get Sally for me, please."

Sally arrived even more somnambulant. "Lady Trent?"

"Help me into one of those black gowns."

"But begging your pardon, you have come out of mourning."

"Never mind that, I have much to do today. And not a word of this to anyone. Do you understand?"

"But what shall I tell Miss Trent? She will surely know that you are gone."

"That I am out and will be back shortly. You can tell her that I will explain when I get back, but that I do not desire any of the other members of the household to know that I have left. As far as they are concerned, I am still resting up after last night's ball. And when I come back to my room, make sure you are the one who answers the summons of the bell."

Althea performed a surreptitious review of the bellpulls in the open parts of the house and a rapid scan of her raven. Then, after a quick bite of toast and a sip of tea Sally brought to her room, Althea affixed one of her old dark bonnets on her head and pulled the veiling down over her face.

She went silently down the stairs and out into the street where she hailed one of the hackney carriages that were already navigating the London streets in search of business. The driver showed some surprise at the sight of a gently bred woman traveling alone at an early hour of the morning, but he refrained from comment. Althea supposed that the drivers of hackney carriages must have seen a great many stranger sights and didn't ask questions so long as the fare was paid.

She had the driver pull the carriage down the street from the Bow Street court, in front of the new Covent Garden. The patrons of the theater had long since retired to their beds, and what was left of the festive performance atmosphere were the beggars and painted ladies whose night's work had allowed them to indulge in the searing pints of gin sold in the district. Fish mongers and apple carts called to anyone who would listen while they rumbled their wares up the cobblestones to the market. Street urchins played in the gutters and shouted to each other as they dodged the horses and carts.

The driver, who was a portly gentleman with a fine set of whiskers and the solid deportment of a man who thoroughly knows his trade, got off the box and came to open the door of the carriage. With the flick of his whip in the air he shooed away some tattered urchins agog to see what strange specimen of humanity might emerge from a carriage at that time of the morning.

"Are you sure you want to leave off here, milady? Begging your pardon, but this area ain't what I'd expect a gentle lady to want to come to at this hour," he said.

"Yes, I have an appointment with the magistrate of Bow Street." And when the driver looked at her in surprise, "No, I am not about to be clapped in irons, my good man. Rather, I wish Magistrate Read to investigate a little matter for me, but do not wish it to be publicly known."

The driver nodded sagely. "Then I will be waiting for you until you comes out."

"Excellent. Ah, I spy a man with a big ring of keys. He must be connected with the court."

Althea stepped down from the carriage and accosted the official. "I must speak with Mr. Read on an urgent matter."

The official looked startled to be addressed by anyone at such an early hour, let alone a lady dressed head to toe in the darkest black. "Magistrate Read don't come until about nine o'clock, madam."

"Is there a place where I may sit and wait for him? It is of the utmost importance that I speak to him before his court duties make private speech impossible."

"There are his chambers. I suppose he wouldn't mind if I let you wait there, seeing as how you are so determined."

"Thank you!" She entered the stone portal of Bow Street. The magistrate's court seemed to be much in the usual style, with a raised platform with a large table from which he could pronounce justice and two low tables below for assorted counsel. Althea imagined that it was not much changed from the wild days of the Fielding brothers. There were also several doors that led off into rooms presumably for court officials, Magistrate Read, and any persons held as prisoners.

The official led her to a heavy oak door behind the dais and, after several tries with a large iron key, opened it enough to allow Althea to pass through. Timid morning light filtered through a dusty window. The chamber had a floor littered with piles of papers and legal tomes. A fireplace on one wall held the ashen embers of a fire. The other walls were lined with shelves and little square cubby holes from which papers stuck out like quills on a porcupine.

Barely visible under all the paper was a small lawyer's desk with a utilitarian wooden chair behind it. Another wooden chair sat to one side with several leather-bound books stacked on top of the seat. The official hurried over and removed the books, placing them on the floor with the others, and gestured toward the chair with his hand. "You may wait here if you please, madam." And then seeming to notice the disorder of the room for the first time, he added, "Beg your pardon, but the charwoman left a fortnight ago, and we've not had time to employ another."

Although Althea was quite sure that the magistrate's chambers had not been cleaned in months, she said, "There is no need to apologize. I perfectly understand. Thank you." She sat down and shook her heavy bombazine skirt out, sending clouds of dust across the plank floor. "Now, you will be so good as to let Magistrate Read know I am here as soon as he arrives, won't you?"

"Aye, madam. I'll do better than that. I'll have a note sent to his rooms that a lady wishes to see him. May I say who?"

"Tell him a widow lady. That should be enough." She pulled a coin out of her reticule and put it into his hand. "Thank you."

The man's eyes lit up at the sight of the money. "Your servant, madam." He bowed reverently and then quietly shut the door behind him.

When Mr. Read arrived an hour later, Althea had examined most of the papers in plain view, read several passages on various legal topics from the books on offer, and taken a survey of the insect carcasses that littered the windowsill. There were three spiders, five houseflies, and a speckled lady bug. She sat down quickly as she heard the door open.

Mr. Read greeted her warmly. "To what do I owe this great pleasure?" He was as rumpled as at their last meeting, with a cravat that was loosely and negligently thrown around his neck, a mottled felt waistcoat, and a fitted coat on which the last button hung down by a thread.

Althea hesitated. Although she had come with every intention of telling him about the thief's actions at the Norwich ball, her courage failed her at the sight of a magistrate of the court. What would he think of her? He would be more than displeased to find out that she had been kissing the criminal she was supposed to catch. He would have no choice but to remove her from the case. Instead she said, "Several things have lately come to pass, and I wished to seek your guidance, sir."

"I would be happy to be of assistance." He shifted some papers around and then sat down behind the desk. If he noticed the chaos around him, he did not show it. "So tell me, Lady Trent: what has transpired?"

"Two servants have disappeared from the Levanwood household, and I suspect some mischief. Whether or not it is connected with the Richmond Thief, I cannot tell."

"His Grace sent me word that your trap failed to produce any results last night."

She nodded, torn again between the truth and mortification. In the light of the morning, her conduct in the library had really been unpardonable. Why, anyone would think she was a common hussy, selling her charms to strangers. No, worse than that, to a thief. And yet, he had sent her away like an honorable gentleman. He could not therefore be so lost and depraved. And more embarrassing still, she had to admit she had enjoyed kissing him back. It was extremely vexing. There was no way she could tell Mr. Read the truth.

"My jewels were not temptation enough," she said.

"Perhaps the thief was otherwise occupied."

Althea blushed, but Mr. Read did not apparently sense it, because he continued, "Another try might be in order. If we could just flush him out in the open and identify him, we would likely prevent further attacks. Then it would be just a matter of time before we brought him to justice." He shook his head, and added, "But what is this you tell me about disappearing servants?"

Althea related what she knew about the valet and Mary and then produced the cord she had found in the garden.

Mr. Read examined it closely. "What do you think this signifies?"

"If Mary did indeed see the body of the valet in the garden, I think that this is a piece of a larger bellpull rope used to kill him by strangulation."

"Have you had a chance to examine the bellpulls in the house to see if perhaps one is missing or cut?"

"I searched this morning, but only in the rooms I have access to. Obviously, the gentlemen's quarters were impossible to search."

He nodded. "Unfortunately, without a body or a request from the family to investigate, I have little reason to send a principal officer to the house."

"At least you have been alerted should a body wash up on the banks of the Thames or something. And I will see what else I can manage to discover. Sometimes idle gossip produces valuable information."

"Servants' gossip often does."

She smiled. "I'm glad we agree. It seems strange to me that people in London appear to treat servants as if they have neither eyes nor ears. They have both, and mouths too, which makes me hopeful that I will soon be able to trace Mary. Then I should be able to get a better description of what she thinks she saw."

"When you do, please send me word. Was that all you wished to discuss?"

"No, but perhaps I am keeping you from your duties?"

Mr. Read pulled a battered watch from his pocket and squinted at it. "It appears I have quite another hour before I must attend to the matters of the day."

"Then I have several questions regarding the prior crimes of the Richmond Thief. His Grace seemed to feel that his crimes varied quite widely in execution, but I had understood from you that was not the case."

Mr. Read nodded. "Here is a point of disagreement between His Grace and I regarding which crimes should be attributed to the thief. Since our initial conversation, I will admit that I have come around to his way of thinking."

"In such cases of doubt, I have often found it useful to consult a third person, whose perspective may clarify certain issues."

"Your ladyship, perhaps?"

"I would be honored indeed if you would allow me to consult any documents you might have related to this matter."

"It would be my pleasure. I had meant to put my notes in order, but my duties as magistrate have prevented me from dedicating the time to it I should have. Here—" He started to dig through the piles, pulling out one paper and another.

Clouds of dust rose from the desk. Althea coughed delicately into her hand. Mr. Read grinned. "Do not suppose that my office in any way represents the state of my faculties. Although it may not appear so, there is a method to my papers."

"I have often observed that the greatest minds do not follow the straightest paths," she said between coughs.

"Just so. A creative approach to crime detection is most effective and the charwoman was let go and we haven't gotten another yet, so this is—ah, yes, here is the last of it." He pulled a sheaf of papers out from the bottom of the pile. A feather fluttered to the ground at Althea's feet. She picked it up.

"My pen!" Mr. Read said excitedly. Althea handed it to him. "The best pen that ever was, Lady Trent. I'm so glad we found it." He pushed the pile of papers together in his hands and then passed them across the desk to Althea.

"Here you are, madam, all the notes on the robberies. As you can see, they are in a bit of a muddle, but they should provide enough for your ladyship's review. If you would be so kind as to return them as soon as you are able, I will have one of my clerks put them together properly."

"Yes, of course. Could I trouble you for a bit of string?"

Mr. Read produced a length of it from the recesses of the desk, and Althea trussed the papers up like a package and then stood, tucking them under her arm. "I must return to Levanwood House before I am missed."

The driver seemed pleased that she had emerged unshackled from her meeting with Magistrate Read and was even more pleased when she told him she would double his fare if he moved with utmost speed. He maneuvered the bulky carriage like a swan through the water, swerving this way and that to take advantage of any opening in the traffic.

Althea had him pull up behind the house, thanked him, paid him handsomely, and then entered Levanwood House from the back door. She was able to make her way to her room without running into anyone of the family. The kitchen maid who saw her was well known to Althea and promised to hold her tongue. Althea tucked her hat and the papers deep into the drawers of the armoire. She pulled the bellpull, secure in the knowledge that she had carried her secret excursion off without a hitch.

Unfortunately, it was the maid Bridgett, not Sally, who appeared.

Althea struggled to hide her annoyance. "I suppose Sally was indisposed?"

"Yes, milady. Mrs. Buxton had urgent need of her."

"Very well. Do help me off with this dress and into one of those muslin ones."

Bridgett gave her an odd look but started to work the buttons at the sleeve.

"I have been out in the back garden, and I find black is much easier to keep clean," Althea said nonchalantly.

Bridgett nodded. She was a stout young lady, no more than eighteen, but with the ease and dignity of a mature woman. "Them fine muslins is awful difficult. One spot and they is ruined."

"So true. I think the current fashions must have been started by dressmakers for the purpose of greater trade."

Bridgett smiled. "Just so, milady."

As she was assisting Althea with the line of small buttons at the back of the dress, Althea, sensing an opportunity, said, "Has any word come from Mary? Although I should never question Lady Levanwood's management of her own household, it is sad to see someone turned off for such a reason. I had considered engaging Mary myself at my house in Somerset, should she desire a change of scenery."

"No, milady, we heard nothing."

"Did she have family in town?"

"I don't know, she never mentioned no one."

"Well, please spread the word that if anyone hears of her, I should like to make her an offer of employment."

"Yes, milady."

"And it was Langley she thought she saw?"

"Yes, she was sure—dragged me all the way out to the yard to see."

Althea shook her head. "Very strange."

"Yes, milady."

"And Mary did not seem like the sort of girl who would make up fantastic stories, but then again, you might know better about that."

"She wasn't, as far as I know. Seemed like a proper brought up girl. Your ladyship wouldn't have to worry about giving her a position. She gave no trouble before the diamonds went missing."

"Yes, those diamonds are a problem. And there wasn't anyone who disliked Mary for some reason, was there? A large house can often foment disagreement."

"Not as I know, milady. She kept to herself, she did."

"I've heard that she's not the first maid turned off from the house. Is that true?"

Bridgett thought a moment and then decided to answer. "I do not know, but there have been other maids that ran off before. Several since I came here, gone without a word to nobody. But Mrs. Buxton told me they was lazy girls, so no loss to anyone."

Althea sat at her dressing table to allow Bridgett to brush out her hair and twist it up in the simple style Althea favored.

"And Mrs. Buxton seemed pleased with Mary's performance? Before the diamonds, I mean."

"Begging your pardon, but Mrs. Buxton don't think nobody does what she ought."

Althea smiled. "She is a strict task master?"

Bridgett nodded. "But she's as fine an abigail as any in London, so she has a right to be particular."

"And is there a Mr. Buxton?"

"Dead these three years, just as I came on with the Levanwood family."

"And he was also employed here?"

"Valet to Lord Charles."

"But not to Lord John? Although I suppose they must have very different requirements for their valets."

Bridgett chuckled, and then recalling herself, coughed delicately. "Yes, milady. My Lord John employs a Frenchman. Calls himself d'Orsay."

"I take it Mr. d'Orsay does not make himself popular?"

"We don't hold with foreigners," Bridgett replied simply. She secured Althea's hair with several long pins and then said, "And your cap, milady?"

"I have several tucked away in the wardrobe." Bridgett went to retrieve one, and Althea added, "I suppose Lord John may hire whom he chooses. He is a dashing young man, after all, and we cannot pretend to understand all the intricacies of masculine fashion."

Bridgett came back to the dressing table with a very pretty lace confection Althea hadn't been able to resist. "As Mrs. Buxton says, *a proper English gentleman should not be at the dressing table more than a girl in her first season.*"

"I had not thought it could be so long."

"Much longer, from what Mrs. Buxton says."

"He is such a fine gentleman, at least the effort is worth the end result."

"He is very handsome," she agreed warily. "But with some unusual habits? I have often seen him out in the garden at night."

"I'm told he sleeps but little and very poorly."

"That would account for it, I'm sure." Althea paused, and then her eyes met Bridgett's in the mirror. She lowered her voice. "I shouldn't pry, of course, but anything you might feel free to tell me, I would be glad to know. Although I am technically a member of the family, I'm afraid I do not know the Levanwoods as I should."

Bridgett responded with a measuring look. Althea's easy concourse with the kitchen staff must have weighed in her favor, because Bridgett sighed and then said, "He's a strange gentleman. Not caring for no one and nothing but himself. There's not a servant in this household but will give him a bad name. That's why he had to bring that Frenchie here. Couldn't get no proper English servant who would take him. Gives me the chills, Lord Bingham does."

"Is he physically abusive to the staff?"

"No, but I hear that there isn't a day where he's not in his cups by midday."

Althea thought about her rides in his high phaeton. "Really? I must say he covers it quite well."

"He would. His mother meaning to have you married."

"Me? Ridiculous."

"Not since your ladyship rejected Lord Charles."

"So the servants know that too? I should have expected as much."

"Yes, milady." Bridgett finished adjusting the cap. "There, milady."

Althea stood. "Thank you. If you wouldn't mind, I will ask to have you come to me always. I find your assistance invaluable."

Bridgett curtsied low. "As you wish, milady."

Althea joined Jane in the blue salon. They had agreed to accompany Cousin Bella on a shopping excursion, but Bella was habitually tardy. Jane sat by the fire actively working a needlepoint that demonstrated both her skill and her tenacious attention to detail. Althea picked up her own indifferent cross-stitch and settled into a chair and easy conversation. They were soon interrupted by the announcement of the arrival of Sir Neville.

That voluble gentleman clapped his hands together as he entered the room. "How charming a picture. Such industry and loveliness! Lady Trent, Miss Trent, you must be complimented on dexterous fingers. I swear I don't know how you ladies do it."

The ladies rose to receive his profuse compliments and then sat again, Althea in her chair and Jane on the settee next to Sir Neville, whose corset creaked happily as he sank down.

"And to what do we owe the pleasure of this visit?" Althea said.

"My dear Lady Trent, I have come on a mission of great importance. With your permission, I have taken a box for this evening at Covent Garden. Only think, the divine Mrs. Siddons as Lady Macbeth, and I have some hope, with the inducement of your charming presence, that His Royal Highness, the Prince of Wales, may favor us at intermission. At the very least, his dear brother, the Duke of York, is sure to make his presence felt."

"A delightful scheme, to be sure." Althea looked over at Jane, seeking some sign of complicity, but Jane resolutely kept to her needlepoint. "Although I cannot speak for Lady Levanwood, I think you may have hit on the only evening this week we are not otherwise engaged."

Sir Neville smiled, his cheeks suddenly pink with happiness. "Then it is settled." He clapped his hands again. "Delightful!"

But just as he pronounced those words, the door opened again. "Beg your pardon"—the butler looked at Althea—"but there is a gentleman come to see your ladyship."

"Indeed?" Althea said. "Show him in, please." Jane looked at her with brows raised.

The butler bowed out and then returned shortly with a stout gentleman of five and twenty, dressed plainly but neatly, with thinning sandy hair and an air of consequence.

"Squire Pettigrew!" Althea and Jane said at once. Sir Neville looked at Jane and then put his ornate quizzing glass up to his eye.

The ladies rose to meet the squire, as did Sir Neville, who levered himself nosily from the settee.

"I did not know you would be in town, sir," Althea said.

"My dear Lady Trent, Miss Trent, I hope I find you well. I have just arrived, you see, and hastened to make my way here to pay respects." He then seemed to notice Sir Neville, who dropped the glass.

Jane said, "May I present Sir Neville Tabard. Sir Neville, this is Mr. Lawrence Pettigrew of Pettigrew Manor in Somerset."

"Quite delighted to make your acquaintance, sir."

Squire Pettigrew replied in kind, but it was clear from his affect that he didn't know what to make of the middle-aged dandy.

Althea invited them all to sit down and noticed that Squire Pettigrew hesitated, waiting to see where she sat. She resumed her prior seat, and he selected the chair next to her.

"May I ring for some refreshment? You must be fatigued from the journey," Althea said.

"No indeed. I brought the carriage, you know, and took it in slow stages. There is nothing fatiguing about that sort of journey, provided the inns are adequate. Although one must always be on the lookout for shifty innkeepers. And there was no need to change horses, so I was happily spared that expense. My horses are steady as they come and can be counted on to take me wherever I need to go. Not that I have reason to travel that much, but still, it is a comfort to have a pair of horses one can count upon not to throw a shoe or sprain a fetlock or some such nonsense."

"And what brings you to London?" Jane said. "For I don't believe you mentioned a journey the last time we had the pleasure of seeing you."

"I have some business with the lawyers that I thought should be attended to in person, matters related to Pettigrew Manor."

"Will your sojourn be of long duration?" Althea asked.

He looked at her intently. "I cannot say."

There was a lull in the conversation, and Althea was just about to remark on the weather or another equally fatuous subject when the door flew open and Lady Levanwood fluttered in. "Oh my dears, sorry to keep you waiting, but I had one of my headaches this morning and you know how low they make me feel. I swear I should never have got up at all, but Buxton had me imbibe some tea and toast and that set me to rights eventually." She stopped, suddenly aware of the gentlemen. "Oh dear, Sir Neville, what a pleasure. And—" She looked inquiringly at Squire Pettigrew.

Althea made the introductions.

"Oh," Lady Levanwood said with a certain elevated hauteur, "and come all the way from Somerset too! Very happy to make your acquaintance."

Pettigrew bowed low. "The pleasure is all mine." Then there was another awkward silence until Sir Neville jumped gallantly into the breach with a description of his theater scheme and a general extension of the invitation to all parties present, including Squire Pettigrew.

The squire seemed to warm to Sir Neville upon the receipt of such a gracious invitation and said to Althea as he left, "Although his appearance is not what one would like to see in a man of such advanced years, still he acts the part of a true gentleman. My mother always said that one should never judge by appearances no matter how one is tempted, and while I find that maxim to be true on most occasions, I am still pleasantly surprised by the affability and condescension of one whom I must otherwise condemn most strenuously as a dandy."

Althea cut in with, "So true," and then thanked heaven that she had the excuse of Cousin Bella's errands to end the interview. Lady Levanwood whisked them off for the express purpose of finding new kid gloves and an ivory fan that she had seen several weeks prior and was now determined to buy.

When Bella was suitably distracted examining a pair of long kid-leather gloves dyed the palest shade of pink, Jane took the opportunity of saying to Althea, "At least in London I thought we might be safe from Pettigrew!"

"Apparently not," Althea replied.

"It's not like him to do anything on a whim."

"Perhaps he sought to keep the visit a surprise."

"Not a very pleasant one," Jane said, "to you or to Cousin Bella. She looked daggers at him, hoping, I suppose, to warn him away."

If that was the case, then Lady Levanwood was sure of disappointment, for Squire Pettigrew arrived punctually and managed to secure a seat next to Althea in the carriage. He took full advantage of this position, speaking to her in a low voice. "I had thought to have private speech with you, Lady Trent, but I find that may be difficult while you are in residence at Levanwood House. I have been informed that persons of fashion parade in Hyde Park, so, once I have had an opportunity to hire a suitable curricle, would you favor me with your company?"

"Why certainly, sir, if I am not otherwise engaged. For you must know that Lady Levanwood has a wide circle of friends, and I am quite at her disposal."

"Of course," he replied, not very well pleased. "One must always place duty above all things. *One's word is one's bond*, my mother always said, and you know how wise dear mother was. You were a great favorite with her, I assure you Lady Trent. *If I could but have such a lady for my dear son*, she'd often say. Of course, that was before the death of Sir Arthur, which, however melancholy an event, must at least have renewed mother's hopes for the future."

Charles, who was seated opposite Althea, called her attention with some remark about the Scottish Play, and Althea gratefully responded, determined, at least for one evening, to keep conversation with Pettigrew at a minimum.

The carriage pulled up in front of the theater, which bore very little resemblance to the sad edifice Althea had previously seen. The building was ablaze with light, and there were carriages of every description jostling with one another to secure a prime location in order to disgorge a bevy of brightly dressed men and women. The drunks and the urchins were nowhere to be seen. All was artifice and pleasure.

Sir Neville met the Levanwood family in the large foyer, under the glittering lights of the chandeliers. He immediately hustled the party, which was complete except for John and the marquess, to his box, on the off chance that the Duke of York or his illustrious brother had come early to the play. Sadly, this was not the case.

Undaunted, Sir Neville entertained his guests with a steady flow of ton anecdotes and gossip. The conversation was interspersed with brief visits from Lady Levanwood's friends, who popped in and out like small brightly colored birds, chirping endlessly about nothing in loud voices. Sir Neville's own wide acquaintance also paid court to the party, and sometimes the box was so filled with noise Althea could barely hear the superficial conversation of the person next to her.

From behind her strategically placed fan, Althea also watched the other theatergoers settle into their seats. Truly, the theater buzzed with human activity. There was Lady Lamb, dressed that evening in a more demure blue silk, seated beside her husband, and the elderly Viscount Rothingham, a great friend of the marquess, ogling the women of lesser morals parading down in the pit, their garish silks and satins shimmering in the flickering light of the chandeliers.

The women's movements reminded Althea of the dance of the honey bees she had observed, back and forth, wiggling their charms for the world to see. Althea noted with a certain detachment that Rothingham wasn't the only gentleman attending the ladies' movements. Quite a number of quizzing glasses were poised to better capture the finer details of the beauties' attributes.

The constant flow of persons in and out of Sir Neville's box did not escape the public's notice either, and Althea observed many heads turned in their direction. She smiled to herself. *And here I am,* she thought, *like the conquering bee queen, surveying my new hive kingdom. Veni, vidi, vici.*

She looked up, shaking off her reverie, and encountered the eyes of the Duke of Norwich staring back at her from the opposite side of the theater. She blinked. He bowed slightly, and she responded with a bob of a curtsey. Then he motioned to another man, who stood beside him. Althea recognized Lord George Verlyn. That gentleman smiled as he bowed. If they had ideas of joining the throng already attendant on the Levanwood party, she did not discern it, because the house lights dimmed, the visitors returned to their positions, and Althea turned her concentration toward the stage.

She had never seen a professional theater production, contenting herself with such amateur theatricals as a confined neighborhood could produce. Needless to say, Mrs. Siddons in her most celebrated role bore no relationship to anything Althea had ever experienced. She found herself gripping the front of the box as the tale of murder and madness unfolded, so lost in the story that it was a shock when the lamps were relit at intermission. She sat back in her chair, disoriented.

The box filled again with other members of the Levanwood and Tabard set, including the very welcome addition of the Duke of York. The Regent's brother was a portly gentleman with a ruddy complexion and engaging, easy manners. Although Lady Levanwood had promised to use her connections to secure Althea's presentation at St. James, the momentous event was delayed indefinitely due to the lack of drawing rooms. Despite this lapse, Althea had been privileged to make the Duke of York's acquaintance at the Norwich ball, where he was so kind as to speak with her for several moments.

This he proceeded to do again, commenting favorably on the deep blue of her evening dress and asking affably how she liked the play. Her impassioned answer made him chuckle ruefully. "Aye, Mrs. Siddons is in fine form tonight. Not that I'm terribly fond of the play. Devilish plot what with witches and whatnot. Turns a man's blood to ice watching that horrible woman wring her bloody hands. Mind you, Shakespeare had the right of it—women are more clever and deadly than ever we men suspect."

Althea smiled. "Should I take that as a compliment to my sex?"

The duke laughed. "Most certainly. Since the time of Eve, women have been our undoing."

"But surely we have all felt the nurturing balm of a mother's love. For that alone, we must forgive all else."

"Spoken like a true mother."

Althea nodded. "I have a son and would gladly sacrifice anything for him."

"Nobly said. However, there are mothers aplenty who would not stand such a test. Why, history is replete with them. Medea comes first to mind."

"I am sure that a thorough search would find examples aplenty on both sides of the argument. I simply meant to illustrate that we are neither so bad nor so good, but merely indispensable."

The duke laughed again. "That you are."

Squire Pettigrew edged closer to the royal personage. He looked at Althea timidly, and Althea, secretly amused at the awe and fear written across his pudgy face, made the proper introduction.

The duke eyed Pettigrew sternly and then, rightly concluding that conversation with him would be tedious, turned away to Sir Neville.

"Never in my life," whispered Pettigrew to Althea, "have I been so honored. Truly, it is a humbling experience to stand in the presence of such greatness. I wonder that you can talk so freely. All maidenly feeling must desire reverent silence."

"Obviously it does not," she said.

Pettigrew seemed unsure of how to reply, so he took a deep breath and began another subject. "I have not been idle today. You will be happy to know that I secured a curricle for my sojourn in London, so that we may partake of the promenade in Hyde Park just as I promised you."

But at that moment, there was a commotion, and two well-dressed men entered the already crowded box.

"The Duke of Norwich," Althea said, not entirely pleased to have to introduce Norwich to Pettigrew.

"And who is that with him?" Pettigrew asked.

"Lord George Verlyn, his brother."

"I see." There was an edge to Pettigrew's voice.

The two gentlemen paid their respects to His Royal Highness and to Sir Neville and then approached Althea. "Lovely to see you again, Lady Trent," Verlyn said. He noticed Pettigrew for the first time. "I don't believe I've had the honor . . ."

Althea presented the squire to both brothers and then added, "Mr. Pettigrew has escaped Somerset for a little town diversion."

"I'm sure you'll find London to your taste," Norwich said evenly.

"Indeed, Your Grace. I have just today hired a curricle to promenade with Lady Trent in Hyde Park tomorrow."

Althea, who could not remember actually agreeing to such a scheme, gave Pettigrew a sharp look.

Norwich paused a moment and then replied, "There must have been some misunderstanding, for I had understood that Lady Trent was engaged to ride with my brother and I for the next several days. Had we not planned it so, Lady Trent?"

Pettigrew remained silent, cowed by the force of personality that had prevented far greater men from wishing to gainsay the duke.

Althea looked at Norwich, her eyes warm with gratitude. "Yes, sir, I believe we had."

Verlyn stepped in, a twinkle in his eye. "Indeed, for you had expressed a desire to see my new curricle, I believe, when we last spoke."

"And your horses," Althea replied. "Cousin John was in such raptures that I have a great curiosity to see such magnificent specimens."

Finally, goaded beyond limit, Pettigrew blurted out, "But you've never been interested in horses!"

Althea turned her wide eyes to him innocently. "In Somerset I had not been privileged to see such fine ones. You must admit there is quite a difference between the farm horse and the thoroughbred."

CHAPTER THIRTEEN

The next morning, Althea dragged Jane out shopping with her so as to avoid being home when Pettigrew called. She also stopped by Madame Longet's for a final fitting of her masquerade costume. It had been decided that Verlyn was to be her escort that afternoon, so as she stood still while the seamstresses pulled and pinned fabric around her, she daydreamed a little about a carriage ride with a charming and handsome man.

He arrived in a smart curricle with a well-matched pair of bays. As he handed her up, he remarked, "I hope the horses don't disappoint."

"Of course not. I want to thank you for your timely intervention. You saved me from one of the greatest bores in Somerset."

"I had no notion," he said ironically. Then, getting up beside her, "Although my knight errant service does give me the opportunity to converse at length with you, which I have desired for some time."

"Beware. Your brother will tell you that my conversation runs to esoteric and not altogether pleasant subjects."

"Really? But then my brother has always been odd, so the unusual is sure to fascinate him."

"More likely repulse. I will refrain from my natural conversation and ask you about your travels. Where is the strangest place you have ever visited?"

"But that is hardly a safe subject, for my conversation may be just as repulsive. Exactly what subjects have raised an objection, by the way, so that I may avoid them?"

"Insects. My husband was a great scholar of them, and your brother seems not to have the same stomach for ghastly tales of decomposition."

"That is hardly sporting of him, is it? Perhaps you and I are better matched, for the strangest place I have ever been was in India, at a Parsi temple, in fact, where the dead are left for the birds to eat."

"How very interesting. And why do they do that?"

"I don't rightly know, but I believe it may have something to do with the cycle of life."

They were quiet for the next several minutes as Verlyn maneuvered his curricle through traffic. Then Althea said, "I should like to travel abroad. We had thought to travel, Arthur and I, but then his health took a turn for the worse, and it was not to be."

"Perhaps when Napoleon is finally routed, you may get your wish."

Althea sighed. "Yes, I can only hope. Although travel is not quite so easy for a woman alone."

Verlyn gave her a sidelong glance and said with a smile in his voice, "Quite ineligible. Then again, I can tell that you are a woman who does not hold much with convention."

"Have I not comported myself with propriety?"

"No breath of scandal has reached me, but I have been absent from society more than I have partaken of it."

"Hardly a ringing endorsement."

He laughed. "You do not need my endorsement, madam. My brother's seal of approval is more than enough."

Upon reaching Hyde Park, they entered into a jovial conversation about travel again, interspersed at random with greetings and side conversations with the other grandees parading themselves along the Serpentine. Althea had never spent such a delightful afternoon. Verlyn's easy manners charmed her, and his sharp intellect, displayed in any number of observations about foreign peoples and places, drew her in. *It is a good thing I have a hard head,* she thought to herself, *or I should be in love with him already.*

As they slowly proceeded back through the park in the direction they had come, they passed the section of the park where she had strolled with Cousin John. When her attention was caught by a flock of ravens circling above a copse of trees a little beyond the walking path, she had half a mind to ask Verlyn to stop the carriage and walk.

Then Verlyn urged his horses forward and made some remark about Poodle Byng. Byng's carriage was just ahead of them, and he had an exquisitely groomed dog perched up beside him where a passenger would normally sit. Althea noted that poodles were considered one of the most intelligent breeds. A discussion of dog breeding ensued, and the opportunity to investigate the ravens was lost. But Althea, studying Verlyn's handsome profile, had some hope that it might be repeated soon.

When they reached Levanwood House, Verlyn said, "I hope we shall meet again soon. Are you attending Lady Shirling's masquerade?"

"Yes, I am. And you?"

He nodded. "But I shan't tell you what my costume is to be, for what fun would it be to know before the unmasking at midnight?"

"I guarantee that you shall never guess mine," Althea replied.

His eyes lit up with amusement. "A challenge, but then you are a lady of your word, so we shall see."

It was only after he had seen her safely inside and she was dreamily untying the ribbons of her bonnet that the truth hit her like a bolt of lightning. *A lady of her word!* That was the phrase the Richmond Thief had used. It was Lord George Verlyn! Oh, the travel now made sense. He would be able to slip in and out of England, and no one would ever suspect. Then again, what did the son of a duke need with money? She had never heard that he was spendthrift, and the Norwich family was known to be rich beyond comprehension, but perhaps the ton had been duped?

Althea hurried to her bedchamber and resolutely shut the door, certain of at least a half an hour of repose before she would call Bridgett to dress her. She sat down heavily on the bed, a thousand thoughts jostling together in her brain. She touched her lips with a gloved hand. And he had been watching her, waiting for just the moment to steal a kiss. But he was more than a thief of love. He was the thief of family treasures, a man who brought misery to all of his victims. That thought depressed her more than she could possibly say.

Jane opened the door. "Finally, you're back," she said, and noticing Althea's expression, "What's happened?"

Althea stood up. She removed her gloves and tossed them on the bed. "Nothing to worry about, dear, I have just been thinking about my monograph. I don't know that it will be enough yet for the Royal Society."

Jane looked at her sharply. "That is not what you were thinking about. Did Lord George do something to upset you?"

"Quite the opposite. Unlike his brother, he is a very charming man. Don't fret, Jane. I will tell you some time or other. But what is it you wished to speak to me about?"

"I wanted to seek your advice. My costume arrived this afternoon, and despite all that trouble, I'm not sure it really suits me."

"A handmaiden to Good Queen Bess not suit you? How could that be? Let me see what wonders Madame Longet hath wrought."

She followed Jane, determined to show appropriate interest, but her mind was still at sea. Lord George Verlyn was the thief! How would she ever disclose such a truth to his brother? She must act as if nothing had happened when she met Norwich on the morrow, and every day after that until she could find a way to tell him properly.

The following afternoon, Norwich arrived promptly at five o'clock. As he handed Althea up into the carriage, she thanked him for his gallantry.

He replied, "It is nothing. One could see from your face how little you welcomed that fellow's invitation. Can't say as I blame you."

Althea sighed. "It was his manner of assuming my acquiescence without asking that set my back up."

Norwich seated himself beside her and took the reins. "And my manner of doing the same produced the opposite effect?"

"Your motive was different. But I shall have to ride with him soon because he haunts the house, and I've quite run out of excuses to be away when he calls."

"You saw much of each other in Somerset, I understand."

"Our neighborhood is not large, so we could not avoid the connection. But he is a good person in his way. His father was much loved. Unfortunately, the father's early death allowed the son to ascend to his rights too soon."

"And you have no desire to become Mrs. Pettigrew," Norwich added matter-of-factly.

"I have no desire to become Mrs. Anyone."

"Ah yes, the bereavement."

Althea looked at him. "I do not fake my grief, sir."

"No, but I think you find it useful."

Althea was about to retort, but then nodded, acknowledging the hit. "Sometimes."

They lapsed into silence and did not speak again until they had reached the park. Norwich said in a low voice, "Mr. Read wants us to try again."

"Again?" And remembering the thief's comment about the Trent family, "I don't think my husband could ever have given me so many jewels. It is not to be believed. And I have quite forgotten to bring the pastes with me this time, so you will have to wait for their return until we meet again."

"Keep them. They suit you. Besides, who would believe they were really yours if you never wear them again? No, this does not involve your jewels, but rather Lady Cartwright's."

Althea looked at him blankly.

"She is that redheaded woman who always wears those enormous feathered turbans."

Althea nodded in recognition. "It's a wonder she can hold her head up at all."

"She must have a strong neck," he agreed with a faint smile. "But that is beside the point. I have it on good authority that she means to attend the Shirling masquerade dressed as the Queen of Sheba, and for that purpose has had that shocking collar of sapphires remade into a crown."

"Mr. Read thinks that the Richmond Thief would steal a crown off the lady's head? No, it is too risky."

"Be that as it may, he wants us to keep an eye on her."

"That should be no small task in a crowded ballroom."

"With two persons, the task should be half as difficult. Now what shall you be dressed as so that I may know you?"

"This is too bad! I had hoped to be a lady of mystery." And then after a moment she added, "But you certainly shall guess it soon enough."

"Why?"

"Of all subjects, it is the most distasteful to you."

"To me?"

"An insect, my dear sir, an insect."

"You jest," and then he caught sight of her wrathful look, "but I'm sure it will be delightful. I will be dressed as the devil."

Althea's brows shot up. "Well, you may call me rude, but I think the devil suits you."

"Only when I'm with you, Althea."

The press of carriages and salutations prevented further speech for the next quarter of an hour, and when they were at last left alone, Althea said, "It is a good thing that you have offered to take me for a drive today. Although I have taken some pains to be seen riding with others, I wouldn't want the world to think you had entirely given me up."

"I had noticed," he replied.

"Had you? I suppose all of London must notice my movements now that you have brought me to the heights of the ton." She smiled. "How Arthur would have laughed and laughed to see me in such a state! He had a great good humor, and he delighted in the ridiculous above all things."

"I don't see that a pretty woman being courted is much fodder for ridicule."

"Thank you for the compliment, but I know that I am not out of the common way. And my connections are not what one would call particularly noble. No, sir, my success, such as it is, must be entirely laid at your feet."

Norwich did not immediately reply, and Althea thought that her sportive manner may have offended him. She stole a quick glance, but his face remained impassive and inscrutable. Then she noticed a movement beyond him. The flock of ravens swooped and circled over the section of the park where Althea had walked with Cousin John. Two days in a row?

"I wonder what?" she said to herself. Then, looking at Norwich, she decided to brave his disapproval. Their relationship would be of short duration anyway. "Would you mind very much to walk with me? I find I miss the healthful exercise of country life."

He had seemed lost in thought, but her request brought him back and he replied, "Of course. Let us make our way over to the walking path." He indicated the very spot she had desired to go.

Unfortunately, the press of acquaintances and the slow movement of the carriages prevented swift action, and it was half an hour later when they finally descended. Norwich handed Althea her parasol, saying, "It is a good thing to walk. I have often told my sister, Lady Bertlesmon, that a brisk walk would do more to aid her health than lying about on the couch fancying herself ill."

"I don't believe I have had the pleasure of seeing your sister in London. Does she not come for the season?"

"Some years. At the moment she is in Bath with my mother and Bertlesmon, attempting to recover from a supposed congestion of the lungs."

"My father was a great believer in the value of steam for such conditions, so perhaps the hot baths shall improve her health."

"What she needs is a husband who doesn't coddle her like a petulant child," he replied.

"You do not feel a husband should bow to the desires of his wife? I think we have previously established that I was in such a marriage. I can tell you that the arrangement works admirably well."

"I shall have to take your word for that. Your father was quite a well-regarded physician, I have come to understand."

"My father was a very great man, and his death was a loss to many people."

"Undoubtedly." Norwich looked at her speculatively. "I think especially to you. Am I right in thinking he gave you most of your education?"

"But for him, I would have had none."

"None?"

"My mother died soon after my birth, and I had no governess."

"That is most remarkable. When did he find the time?"

"Every day there was some new knowledge to impart, some moment for instruction. And I am an avid reader, so his library provided what he could not supply. Besides, by the time I reached ten years of age, my duties as his assistant provided an infinite opportunity for learning of the most valuable kind." She paused and looked at Norwich to see if that disclosure had shocked him. He certainly stared at her with a fixed intensity.

Then he smiled. "If you could have traded with my poor sister for a day, what a change that might have wrought."

Althea smiled in return, strangely relieved. "I was certainly not idle. Papa would never have permitted it."

They walked on in silence, Althea silently guiding him out of the prying eyes of the multitude and toward the solitude of the copse of trees. She looked up several times to measure the pattern of the ravens' flight. Then, seeing several swoop down into the brush around the trees not two yards from the walking path, she shut her parasol with a snap, looped it over her arm, picked up her skirts, and charged into the brush.

Norwich stood stunned for several seconds and then came after her. "Althea, my God, what are you about?"

"Science," she called back over her shoulder.

"What?" He caught up with her and tried to grab her arm.

She twitched away. "I have to know what is drawing such a large flock of birds. Ten to one it is a dog or some other poor creature—" And then she stopped and poked the point of her parasol at a small object in front of her. The raven that had been perched on top of it cawed loudly and flew upward with a flap of black wings. "Oh my goodness."

"What?" Norwich leaned over her shoulder.

Slowly, very slowly, Althea bent down and used her parasol point to turn over the object—a hand, gnawed upon and held together by ragged strings of dry skin and sinew. The smell of death wafted up, poisoning the air around them. A cloud of flies emerged from the bracken and hovered over the hand possessively.

Norwich jumped back. "My God, what?"

But Althea wasn't listening. She crouched down, moving slowly from the spot where the hand lay, digging as best she could, removing dirt and leaves carefully with her gloved hands. First a handless arm emerged, clothed in stiff black fabric. She continued on, burrowing into the sandy soil, and then suddenly she stood up. "Look, Norwich."

A distorted and discolored object that had once been a face, but was now darkened beyond recognition, stared back at Norwich. He clapped a hand over his mouth, his forehead wet and his skin ashen.

Althea looked back at him. "May I infer that your work with Bow Street has never involved the discovery of a corpse?"

He shook his head mutely.

"It appears I have the advantage of you. Come help me, please. Although animals have done some of the work in digging it up—note the way the hand has been pulled off and gnawed upon—I don't have enough yet to be able to—oh dear."

"What?" he croaked.

Althea pointed to the dark clothing. "It's a maid's uniform." She crouched down again, pulling away at the collar at the throat of the corpse until the darkened skin of the neck could be seen. "It appears she was strangled. Look, there is still a piece of ribbon clinging to the flesh. And see how the neck has been torn and compressed here? Fortunately, the dry soil has prevented more advanced putrefaction."

"I'll take your word for it." He produced a handkerchief and mopped his brow.

She pulled at the fabric once more, and insects of every description, startled midfeast, ran over her gloved hands. She stood, cradling a spiny worm in her palm.

"Our very own beetle!" She held it out to Norwich in her excitement.

Norwich looked down at her hand for a second and then away. "We must alert Bow Street," he said quietly. "Come, Lady Trent, you have done enough." He held out his hand imperiously and turned away. She slipped the larva into her reticule and reluctantly allowed him to guide her back to the carriage.

"Hutchins," Norwich called to the tiger slowly walking up and down with the horses, "there has been a terrible accident, and we are off to get help. Please stay by that clump of trees over on the far side of the walking path and make sure no one enters the area. We shall be back directly."

Hutchins nodded, seemingly unperturbed by his master's ashen look and his companion's disreputable appearance. "Of course, Your Grace."

When they arrived at Bow Street, Norwich insisted on entering. He handed her the reins, saying, "Have no fear, they should be quiet enough for a minute or two. There now, maintain a firm grip. I shall be out directly."

Althea sat in the carriage, holding the reins as firmly as she could, contemplating her stained dress and ruined gloves and turning the discovery of the body over in her mind. She had not been willing to say it aloud, but there stood a good possibility that the body in the park and the missing Mary were one and the same. And that could mean only one thing—there was a murderer living in Levanwood House.

Norwich returned to the carriage in less than two minutes and took the reins from her.

"So?" Althea said.

"Read shall see to it and bring Hutchins around."

"And us?"

Norwich looked down at her and then smiled reluctantly. "I had not thought about it. Your reputation may not survive a return in my company looking like that."

"I knew I should not have thrown off the black dresses," she said. "They are so forgiving with stains."

Norwich chuckled, the tension leaving his face. "I had never contemplated the benefits of widowhood in just such a light."

"It is one of the few benefits, so one must take full advantage. Do you think this murder is connected to the Richmond Thief?"

"Unlikely," Norwich replied. Althea debated whether to mention her suspicions regarding Levanwood House, but she thought better of it. What could Norwich do, after all? And if the Richmond Thief were indeed Lord George, Althea could not imagine such a man murdering two innocent servants. Nothing made any sense anymore. She would have to speak with Read herself.

Norwich maneuvered the carriage back into traffic.

"Where are we going? Lady Levanwood will expect me back to dress for supper."

"Norwich House, where you will clean yourself up as best you can. I'll send a note around to let Lady Levanwood know that we have been unavoidably detained."

"By what?"

"Eating Gunter's ices or some other equally frivolous activity."

Althea nodded. "That sounds like a good plan."

"I'm glad at least in that we agree. And then perhaps we can arrange another moment for a conversation of a more serious nature."

Althea looked at him. What could that mean? Probably a lecture on the propriety of women engaging in insect studies, criminal investigation, and corpse discovery. "Of course, if you wish it."

"I do," he replied, but he would not say more.

Althea returned to Levanwood House with her face washed and her hair tidy. She had discarded the gloves and shaken the loose dirt from her gown. She was prepared with a story about tripping and falling outside Gunter's, but the Levanwoods had all retired to dress for supper. Althea called for Bridgett and then proceeded to tell her the story. Bridgett eyed the dress. "'Tis such a pity, but I will see what the washerwoman can do. Or perhaps the dress may be re-made with a different skirt."

Jane was another matter. Her sharp eyes detected a plot, and she could only be placated by a sincere promise to disclose all when the ladies retired to bed. It was only after fobbing off Jane and completing her toilette with Bridgett that Althea remembered the beetle larva in her reticule.

She emptied the reticule's contents on the counterpane, and the spiny creature fell with them, wriggling to and fro. She studied it for several moments and then dashed for the armoire, pulling out items until she unearthed the pages of her husband's notes. She leafed through them, running her finger over the tables of calculations. Indeed. But the timing wasn't right. Then she had a sudden flash of insight. The raven. Of course. She picked up the larva and watched it squirm delicately in her palm.

"We may understand all things if we just examine them scientifically," she said to herself. "Nature never lies."

CHAPTER FOURTEEN

The morning of the masquerade, several large boxes arrived bearing the name of Madame Longet's establishment. Althea had the boxes carried to her chamber for a private inspection. What with writing and submitting her manuscript to the Royal Society, accompanying Lady Levanwood to any number of society events, and frequent costume fittings with Madame Longet, Althea had been unable to slip away to speak in person with Magistrate Read. Instead, they had corresponded by short notes sent back and forth by small errand boys employed for the purpose.

Although skeptical at first, Read had soon come around to Althea's way of thinking on a number of points. However, Althea had not yet explained to him the mechanism by which she could with certainty determine that the victim had died of strangulation at least five weeks before. That meant that the victim couldn't be Mary. So one problem was solved, but another remained.

Jane joined Althea in her chamber, anxious for the unveiling of Althea's unusual costume. "I still think Madame Longet may be declared a genius if this costume retains any beauty at all. What you were thinking in picking such a thing, I will never understand."

"The beauty of the costume is of little interest to me. One cannot expect a masquerade costume to enhance one's beauty, after all. The point is to be hidden from view, is it not?"

"A smart woman attempts to do both."

"But you know I couldn't back down from a challenge." Althea lifted the lid of a large square box. "This must be the headpiece. Do help me, please."

The ladies tussled with the fine layers of paper wrapping until Althea could finally pull it free. "There," she said triumphantly. The headpiece was in the shape of a close-fitted turban with a fabric mask over the eyes that fastened by means of ribbon loops attached to concealed buttons on the turban. The mottled appearance of the beetle was created by a series of interwoven feathers—gold, brown, and black—with a layer of silver-threaded tulle stretched over it so it shimmered in the light.

"That is much better than I imagined," Jane said, "but how shall you wear your hair? It seems too tight a fit to twist your hair up the way you have been wearing it."

"Hmm." Althea studied the turban a moment. "I suppose it shall have to be down my back a la your glory days. But without powder, of course—I should look a fright with powder."

"I don't suppose one could even find it nowadays with the strange immoral times we live in," Jane replied wryly.

The ladies attacked the largest parcel and finally pulled a shimmering garment from its paper folds. Althea held the dress up for Jane to see. It was a simple gown of wheat-colored satin cut to skim the body. The beetle's carapace was simulated with an overlapping appliqué of black and brown satin circles. An overskirt of the silver tulle gave the same shimmery effect as on the turban. At the back, the tulle cascaded from the shoulders, forming a pair of diaphanous wings.

"Again, much better than I had thought," Jane said. "I foresee that you may yet be the belle of the ball, Madame Beetle."

"Unlikely. However, I will admit that I am just a little anxious that it fits properly. Madame Longet was forever pinning it."

Jane patted her arm. "Never fear. Do you wish to try it on?"

"I do not have time this morning, and the night will come soon enough. In any case, there is no going back now."

But the night seemed far away as Althea sat in the blue salon with Jane, drinking tea and nibbling on a honey cake. The day of reckoning could not be postponed. Squire Pettigrew had come to call, and the ladies of Dettamoor Park must suffer the consequences.

"I hear you are gone to a masquerade tonight," Pettigrew said, a large crumb of cake dangling inelegantly from the corner of his mouth.

"Yes," Althea replied, her eyes unable to focus beyond the crumb.

He shifted ponderously in the chair. "Far be it from me to question anything you do, Lady Trent, but I have it on good authority that these masquerades are not quite the thing."

"Um?" Althea replied, still distracted. How could he not feel the crumb when he spoke?

Pettigrew turned imploringly to Jane. "Surely you agree with me on this point. A lady of your years and experience must see how ineligible such a thing is."

"Just how old do you think I am?" Jane said.

"I meant no offense, Miss Trent. You are quite a spritely lady to be sure. I simply—"

"I think we all know what you meant," Althea cut in, finally roused from her crumb contemplation, "but the fact is that Lady Shirling is a great friend of Lady Levanwood, so we had best brave the scandal and go."

"I think upon reflection you will come to see that I am correct. Although she seems amiable enough, I cannot say that I find in Lady Levanwood's conversation and tastes that strict attention to morality that one would hope to see from a leader of society. As I'm sure you would agree, Lady Trent, it is the responsibility of us all to maintain the moral tone of society. My mother always said—"

"And this observation is based on what, pray tell?" Jane said.

"I took great pains to engage her ladyship in conversation at the theater. When I commented unfavorably upon some of the more colorful ladies stationed down by the stage, her ladyship did not join in my condemnation."

"Indeed?" said Althea.

Pettigrew sat up straight in the chair and pursed his lips twice, the crumb bobbing solemnly in time. "No, she merely laughed and said that young men must have some occupation until they marry." He looked at Althea triumphantly. "Can you believe it?"

"Oh yes," Althea replied, enjoying herself for the first time since Pettigrew's arrival. "It seems very sensible coming from a mother of three sons. Not that I would want young Arthur to spend his fortune maintaining a mistress, but I am sure he will have his adventures like all young men when they come of age. The only pity is that young women are not given the same license. In any case, it doesn't follow that Lady Levanwood's views on this issue would lead her to be a poor chaperone for Jane and me." Althea smiled at Jane. "For as you have already pointed out, Squire Pettigrew, we are not green girls just launched upon our first seasons."

Pettigrew puffed his cheeks in and out, letting the crumb fly free once and for all. "Well," he said in an agitated voice. "Well." He took a sip of tea to steady his nerves, and then he chuckled consciously and with some effort. "I had forgotten what a delightfully sportive manner you have, Lady Trent. I am sure that your wit and playfulness account for the many accolades you have received upon your arrival in London." He leaned in as if to impart a secret. "My sources inform me that the Duke of Norwich is quite smitten."

If he had sought to receive either a confirmation or denial, he was disappointed.

"I had not heard such a rumor," Althea replied placidly. "You must understand that I receive a great many invitations from a great many people. As you have seen, my schedule is very full."

"Such a whirlwind of activity, and yet I think the country pleasanter than town." He looked to Jane for confirmation.

"Not necessarily," Jane replied. "I'm sure you will agree that each has merit enough."

"So true," added Althea. "I shared your opinion at first, Squire Pettigrew, but I fear that my first impression may have done the city a disservice. There are delights enough if one takes the trouble to look for them."

Pettigrew sipped his tea, unsure of how to proceed, but if he formed a new plan of attack it was for naught, because at that moment Lady Levanwood bustled in.

"Oh, there you are, dear cousins. I have just got the packages from Madame Longet, and what do you think? After three fittings the bodice will not button! I cannot imagine what must have happened! It is a disaster of the greatest proportions. Come, perhaps you may be clever enough to tell me what must be done." She caught sight of Pettigrew and added, "Ah, the good squire come to call. I am afraid that I have interrupted a pleasant conversation. No doubt you wish to discuss Somerset matters, but I beg you to postpone the discussion. As you can see, the matter of the costume is most pressing!"

The squire bowed over her hand. "Lady Levanwood, I would not dream of detaining the Dettamoor Park ladies further." He gave a speaking look to Althea. "Dear Lady Trent, Miss Trent, I shall hope to have the pleasure of your company for a ride in Hyde Park. Should Tuesday be acceptable?"

Caught, Althea and Jane were forced to assent. Then the squire took his leave, looking entirely too pleased with himself. Once the door closed behind him, Cousin Bella sighed. "It's a wonder he ever decided to come to London, such a prosy, stiff fellow. Well, my dears, now that we are rid of him, you must come with me. It is the most vexing thing imaginable to be thus situated. And I had such hopes for the masquerade!"

The problem of the dress was solved with loops of fabric that extended the range of the buttons to the required circumference. And with that drama behind them, the delights of the evening lay before the Levanwood household with unimpaired splendor. The family dined early and quietly and then repaired to their chambers to dress. Bridgett, who had replaced Mrs. Buxton in all things, curled Althea's long hair with irons from the fire and assisted her into her gown. Once the last button was fastened, Althea looked at the glass. "Oh dear!" she said. "I should have tried the dress on when Lady Levanwood indicated that her costume would not fit."

"But it does fit, milady," Bridgett said.

Althea studied her reflection in the looking glass. "It is a case of fitting rather too nicely than not at all."

She tapped on Jane's door, seeking her advice, but Jane called back, requesting immediate assistance. When Althea opened the door, she found Jane and Sally wrestling with the fabric-wrapped circumference of a monstrous farthingale.

"Good Lord," Althea said with a giggle. "And I have heard Queen Bess's England called a Golden Age. Much the male writers of history know of such things!"

Jane was not amused. "Stop your laughing and help me get this thing around my waist!" Bridgett hurried over, and between Bridgett, Sally, and Althea, the skirt of Jane's costume was finally secured. This was followed by a stiff brocade bodice, cut low and square over her bosom.

"That is daring," Althea said.

"Not as much as you would think. Here, Bridgett, please bring me that ruff," Jane said.

Bridgett picked the circle of stiff linen frills up off the bed. "'Tis a wonder they could move at all with such clothes," she said.

"Not well," added Althea.

The ruff was affixed, and then Jane turned toward Althea. "What do you think?"

"Lovely. Stiff clothes become you, Jane."

"And fitted ones become you." She looked at Althea critically and then dismissed the servants for a moment. "I don't think I've even seen a dress cut so precisely to the figure. Can you even walk?"

"Yes." Althea bit her lip. "But it is so much tighter than the last fitting. I don't know what Madame Longet was thinking. They will all say I am another Lady Lamb!"

"Nonsense. Besides, you will be masked. Although it is a good thing Arthur isn't here to see you."

Althea laughed reluctantly. "He would have been too preoccupied with the realism of the costume to notice much else."

"I doubt any of your admirers will give a second thought to realism."

"At least I am wearing a dry petticoat." Althea made an effort to shake off her anxiety. "It was the challenge of the thing, you see. Norwich was so horrified by my beetle studies that I wanted to show him that all of nature's creatures can be beautiful."

"And tempt him into making you an offer?"

"You of all people know that to be false."

"Oh Althea, what am I to do with you?" Jane smiled knowingly. "Charles will not like it."

"I didn't need a dress to tempt him. My fortune was more than enough."

"Perhaps his feelings run deeper than you know."

"Perhaps. Although it is odd, Jane, he hasn't pressed me of late."

"A man cannot withstand constant rejection."

"I am not wishing him to renew his attentions, I assure you, but it makes me wonder just what he is thinking. Maybe he has decided to give John the floor."

"Our cousins aside, there must be some young buck who has tickled your fancy."

Unconsciously a blush stole up Althea's cheeks. No, her attraction to the thief was too embarrassing to confess to Jane.

"Althea, I demand to know what you are about!"

"I am just attempting to follow your advice and enjoy the season I never had."

When the ladies appeared downstairs, Althea had taken the precaution of throwing an opera cape of rushed satin over her ensemble. It would be prudent to forestall any commentary until she was safely masked. Cousin John, who had dressed more quickly than the ladies, was resplendent in a medieval tunic and a wolf's head mask. Charles had opted for a simple black domino and silken face mask, but he entered into the discussion of the family costumes with enthusiasm. Jane, her hair pulled up and arranged stiffly around a wire circlet and stuck through with a set of pearl hairpins that had been a gift from her late mother, received the most praise.

Charles exclaimed, "You are to be complimented on such a wonderful disguise! It is like stepping backward in time."

He was equally warm when his mother descended the stairs dressed as a country shepherdess, albeit one with the budget for satins and lace. In her hand she carried a silk-covered staff with a cascade of colored ribbons at the top.

"Why, thank you, Charles, although had I known that your brother would come as a wolf, I might have chosen differently. What are my poor sheep to do? Really John, you gave me quite a fright just now!"

John growled menacingly and then laughed.

Lord Levanwood appeared dressed simply like Charles in a blue domino. "Let's get this over with," he said gruffly.

Given the width of Jane's costume, the ladies were squeezed into the carriage, a tumble of satin and legs, while the men rode together in John's phaeton. At the ball, they quickly dispersed in an attempt to find their own set among the riotous atmosphere that already pervaded the ballroom. Althea repaired with Jane to the cloakroom to assist in the adjustment of the now cockeyed farthingale. Once Jane was put to rights, Althea removed her cloak and bravely handed it to a waiting woman. It was now or never.

Jane chuckled as they walked arm and arm into the ballroom. "What a picture we must make—old-fashioned prudence and modern indecency."

"I'd much have preferred artifice and nature," Althea replied. Now that she was actually out in public, facing the sidelong glances of masked men, her confidence had begun to falter once more.

Jane sensed her hesitation. "Do not fret. The costume is not half so daring as those of some of the women here tonight. And if one cannot be daring at a masquerade, then one has no sense of adventure."

Althea smiled, relieved. "What would I do if I did not have you, dear Jane?"

"Live a very boring life."

They moved forward into the crowd, coming near Cousin Bella, who was chattering away to a Celtic princess and a medieval knight. Bella looked over, waved, and then went back to her conversation. The musicians commenced a reel, and a line of dancers formed down the center of the room. Jane and Althea hovered on the periphery, each scanning the crowd, but with different objects.

They were soon approached by a plump courtier dressed in the style of King Charles. He made a low bow, saying, "Fair handmaiden of Good Queen Bess, would you do me the honor of the next dance?"

"Ah, Sir Neville," Althea said before Jane could reply, "I must congratulate you on such a fine costume, but how did you know it was us?"

"Such beauties are not to be hidden so easily, Lady Trent, and I would know Miss Trent in any disguise."

"Very pretty," Jane replied. "I will do my best in the next dance, Sir Neville, but I'm not sure how anyone managed to dance with these great hoops."

"The elegance of your movements shall overcome the ungainly quality of your costume," Sir Neville said. "But we must not neglect Lady Trent. Here, I see good Sir Pennicott over by the wall. Let me make the introduction."

"No need," a familiar voice said from behind the little group. "I will engage Lady Trent, if she will have me."

Althea turned around and found herself staring at a handsome gentleman dressed in a Roman toga. He wore a laurel wreath on his head and a black silk mask over his eyes, and he carried a staff with a metal figure of a lightning bolt at the top. "Lord George?"

He bowed low. "Lady Trent, I believe we have both lost our costume wagers."

"The voice cannot be disguised," she said, hoping to catch a reaction, but she could detect none. "However, we might still be able to carry on. Might I guess that you are dressed as the all-powerful Jupiter?"

He smiled. "I see you have not neglected the study of the ancient myths. Yes, I am the king of Mount Olympus, but you," his eyes traveled slowly up and down her body, "are not the fair Juno."

Althea felt a strange shiver of excitement. "No, Lord George."

He studied her a moment longer. "I cry pardon, for I cannot make it out. What does your costume represent?"

"One of God's most humble creatures, the lowly beetle."

"Extraordinary. You have wrought beauty from disgust."

Althea smiled with real pleasure. "Thank you. That is just as I would wish."

The reel ended, and the next set began to form. Althea, feeling more confident, let Jane and Sir Neville drift away. Verlyn entertained her with light conversation, and upon handing his staff to an attendant, he took her hand and led her on to the floor. The time passed quickly in between the movements of the dance and his witty conversation. When it ended, Althea found herself with a strange sense of disappointment.

A man in a green domino solicited her hand next, followed by a black domino, who turned out to be Cousin Charles.

"Are you enjoying the dance, cousin?" His voice was light.

"Yes. The costumes are wonderful, don't you think?"

"Some are, yes." He turned and then, coming back through the steps of the dance, added, "Yours is indeed a revelation."

Althea didn't like the tone of his remark. "Does a beetle offend you?"

"It's not the subject matter, madam."

"I'm sure I don't know what you mean, sir."

"Come, let us not argue in public. You know as well as I do that your costume is not decent. Indeed, I thought you had better sense than to expose yourself thus."

"The cut of my gown is merely an imitation of a beetle's rounded carapace, dear cousin. Madame Longet made the final adjustments without my knowledge. When it arrived, it was too late to change. Besides, if your mother has not thought to comment on it to me, I think I may brave your disfavor."

"My mother is a silly woman who does not know her own interests, let alone those of the family." The bitterness of his voice shocked Althea. She was happy to take a turn away from him.

When they came back together, he took her arm, smiled, and said softly, "Might I suggest that your willingness to dress the part of the temptress indicates that your grief has abated such that my addresses may be renewed with fervor?"

Althea, at a loss as to how to repulse him, said, "I looked for realism in a costume and had not considered any other aspects. If its fit offends you, I would direct your ire toward Madame Longet."

Charles chuckled. "Come now, since the time of Eve, women have ever been aware of the power they have over us poor men. You knew exactly what you were about. We cannot be blamed for our actions."

Althea turned away without a reply. Upon meeting him again, she remained silent. Charles seemed to study her, and then he said, "If you have thoughts of catching Norwich, let me be the first to warn you that paltry methods such as these will not suffice. Quite the opposite, I'm afraid. The Norwich family is very particular in matters of etiquette. The duke's mother would not like to see such a display from the woman who would take her place, and Norwich has shown no inclination to marry to disoblige his family."

"Thank you, Charles, for your sound advice, but as I have no intention of catching Norwich, I think I may brave the potential displeasure of his mother."

"And Lord George Verlyn?" he said softly. "Remember, she is mother to both."

"Again, I am indebted to you for your knowledge of the peerage, but you may rest assured that I have no such intentions."

Charles merely laughed.

The dance mercifully ended, and Althea found the first opportunity to escape Charles by pretending to discover a rip in her costume that needed instant repair. She walked back to the cloakroom, determined to compose herself before braving the ballroom once more. She seemed to be failing on all counts; she was stung by Charles's reproof and unable to locate either the Queen of Sheba or the Norwich devil in the mass of colorful costumes.

The cloakroom was abuzz with women whose costumes were in various states of adjustment and alteration. The attendants fluttered to and fro like butterflies, ministering to the flower of London society. Here a tear was mended, there a cool compress applied to an overheated forehead, and across the room a lady shrieked, "I've lost my earring," only to be hushed when Althea spied the earring on the ground near her feet.

Althea sank heavily into the only empty chair. In the chair next to her sat a very large woman dressed as the Queen of Hearts. She fanned her reddened face. "Lord what a crush! I've never had to repair to the cloakroom merely to sit down."

Althea nodded. "Indeed."

"And this costume's so heavy. Next time I will come as a sprite—some costume made of gauze." She lifted her full skirt, showing a puffy foot held tight by a satin slipper. "Not this brocade. My Lord, I don't know what I was thinking!" She seemed to notice Althea's costume for the first time. "You certainly have the right of it. What exactly are you? Woodland nymph?"

"Beetle."

"Oh, that is original. Come stand so that I may see."

Althea complied self-consciously and then sat back down.

"Good for you," the lady said approvingly. "One should always take full advantage of one's assets." She smiled in a good-natured way. "I'm sure a lady like yourself would never credit it, but I was once as slim as a willow switch. Should have taken better advantage then! However, my husband doesn't seem to mind, so I guess I can't repine. And children are great ruiners of one's figure, bless them. Have you any children?"

"One," replied Althea.

"Oh, that explains it then. I've seven living and two that died, poor dears. All out of the schoolroom now."

"You must find it lonely. My son is but eight, but I dread the moment when he must be off to school."

"One becomes accustomed to having one's life back. Not that a mother's work is ever done. There always seems to be one or another of them hanging about the house, but at least the girls are finally married off. I never thought to have so much trouble as I did finding suitable husbands for them all. A girl's idea of what makes a good husband bears no relationship to reality. They want these dark romantic types, and yet I ask you, what good is a handsome rake when one has children to feed? Ten to one he will have wasted all of his money on drink and cards. Not that I am opposed to cards—my husband is off enjoying himself with the faro table as we speak—but one cannot live on debt alone."

"Very true. However, it must be hard for a young lady, raised on romantic tales from the circulating library, to accustom herself to reality."

"Yes, but as we know, marriage is all about making the best of the circumstances. These so-called love matches just lead to disaster."

Althea sighed. Her companion was right. It would be best if Althea put all thoughts of love out of her head, particularly since those thoughts ran to a certain disreputable thief. A common rake would have been a better choice. She desired to turn the conversation, so she said, "I have come to understand that faro is quite a popular game. I never had the opportunity to play."

"Don't play unless you have learned. It is not a game for triflers. I've been told that Levanwood is holding the bank tonight, and everyone knows that he is not above turning the play to his advantage."

"Really? Someone told me that the bank always wins. It made me wonder why anyone ever played."

"Oh, in the long run that is quite true, but from night to night one must have the capital to sustain staggering losses. But never fear, my husband knows his limits, and faro is very pleasant in its way."

"Does Lord Levanwood often enact the role of banker?"

The lady nodded. "However, I believe that this is the first time he has done so this season. Finally escaped the wifely harness, poor man. But there, my husband tells me that I should keep my sharp tongue in my head—not that I can help it!" She flicked her fan twice and then struggled to her feet, shaking the full skirt of her costume out. "I must be getting back."

Althea stood as well. "It has been lovely to meet you, Queen of Hearts."

"And also you, Madam Beetle. Perhaps we shall meet again at the unveiling."

"I should like that."

When Althea returned to the ballroom, she noticed a tall devil skulking in a corner. Hoping that she had identified the correct devil, she approached. The man remained silent until she was close enough that others would not hear their conversation. "Althea," he said. His eyes were inscrutable behind the mask.

"My lord," she replied, relieved that she had not confused the matter.

"You have proved the point."

"And what point was that?"

"If you do not know, then I shall certainly not enlighten you." He smiled enigmatically.

"Why not?"

He seemed as if he were to answer, but thinking better of it, he turned away, saying, "Have you located the Queen of Sheba?"

"No."

He scanned the ballroom from his superior height. "I don't think she has yet arrived."

"What are we to do while we wait?"

He held out his arm. "I'm in no mood for dancing. Come, take a turn with me about the room."

"I don't think we will get very far in this crush," she replied, placing her hand lightly upon his sleeve.

"Then let us at least seek refreshment."

Althea nodded. They moved through the crowd with greater ease than anticipated, Norwich's height giving him an advantage in navigation. Soon they reached an antechamber arranged with several long tables for lemonade, claret, and champagne. The crowd was still thick, so they drank their glasses down hurriedly and left, making their way down the hall until they reached a small sitting room lit only by a fire dying in the grate.

Norwich indicated that they should enter, and Althea complied saying, "Surely I shall have to do penance for a year of Sundays if I follow the devil into a darkened room."

"Your soul is safe with me tonight."

She sank down in a chair beside the fire. "This is nice."

Norwich took the chair opposite, moving his cloth tail out of the way before he sat down. "These events can be very tiresome."

They were silent for several minutes, and then Althea said, "So what is the plan for this evening? Shall we orbit the Queen of Sheba until something happens?"

"That was my idea. Do you have another?"

"No, I suppose not." She eyed his profile, wondering if he had any suspicion about the activities of his own brother. "If we had a list of suspects, it might aid our surveillance. Has Magistrate Read ever proposed any to you?"

Norwich turned his head to look at her. "No, unfortunately not."

"Um." Althea turned back to the fire.

"I should think any person who approaches Lady Cartwright would be considered one."

"Any person? Are you considering women suspect as well?"

"Unlikely, I agree, but the thief could employ an accomplice."

"The thief could easily be a woman. In fact, a woman would have greater opportunity. There are places that Lady Cartwright may go that a man could not follow."

"A woman cannot travel as easily as a man."

"She would not need to travel if she had the appropriate accomplice," Althea replied.

"Mr. Read has thoroughly explored the possibility, but even with Bow Street's connections in the basest part of London, Read cannot find any information about smuggling the jewels out of the country. That leads me to believe the thief must take it all upon himself."

"So all men are suspect, but how shall we know who is who? Disguise is the point of a masked ball."

"We must keep a sharp eye," he said.

"Then perhaps it would be best to return to the ballroom."

"Permit me a moment longer."

She eyed him suspiciously. "To rest?"

"No, I am not yet so old. Do you realize that we have spent nearly a quarter of an hour in each other's presence without a quarrel?"

"That long? You must be taking my advice."

He refused the bait. "And what shall you do when the season is over? Return to your fields and streams?"

"Undoubtedly. What pleasures can compare to fields and streams?"

"I'm sure I can think of a few."

Althea gave him a wry look. "Likely not fit for a lady's ear."

"You are unlike any lady of my acquaintance."

"But even I may blush to hear what young men do when they go upon the town. Not that I have any illusions on the score, mind you."

"I'm glad we at least agree on my youth." He studied her face, and Althea felt an unwanted blush steal up her cheeks.

"What holds you back, then?" he said.

"From what?" she replied.

"Forming an alliance."

Althea sighed. Of course Norwich just meant to be difficult. She gave him her most disdainful look. "Is that what they are calling it in London? To be perfectly frank, I believe you are the only gentleman to have the effrontery to mention such an arrangement."

"I won't be the last."

It was just like him to needle her. She replied calmly, "I'm sure, and if it were up to me alone, I suppose I might consider some discreet arrangement, but I have the credibility of my son's name to consider. One cannot be an embarrassment to one's offspring. At least, not very often."

"Many widows, and married women in general, I dare say, would not agree with you."

Althea hoped to give him back his share. "They may do as they please. But don't tell me that you have made a study of such females. I had rather thought from general accounts that actresses were your fancy. I think that is wise. Entangling oneself with other men's wives leads to complications. And widows can be so depressing. Besides, your family does not crave scandal, I understand."

Instead of reacting angrily, he smiled. "Does nothing disturb you? I begin to wonder if there is any topic of conversation that can put you to the blush."

"I have yet to find one, but please continue to try. It keeps our conversation from going stale. And the general consensus is correct, is it not?"

"Why does it matter to you?"

"Merely to an illustration of your character," she said.

"The rumors have been greatly exaggerated."

"They usually are. But you should do what you can to fan the flames. It softens the general impression and makes you seem more mortal."

"I hardly think anyone perceives me a god, Althea."

"No, more like the devil," she replied archly.

At that, a milkmaid with a cockeyed wig and a cloven-hoofed satyr tumbled into the room, too drunk and too absorbed in a passionate embrace to notice that the room was already occupied. Norwich grabbed Althea's hand and pulled her up. "Come, fair beetle, we should be about our business."

They returned to the ballroom just in time to see the Queen of Sheba ascend the stairs. "Look sharp," Norwich said, and then they parted, not to meet again for the rest of the evening. Instead, Althea quietly monitored the queen's crown and did so more particularly when Lord George chanced to approach. All in all it was dispiriting work, and several minutes before the unmasking, Althea slipped away from the ballroom and the intense heat that a room full of costumed dancers produced.

She mopped her brow with a slightly soggy handkerchief pulled from the chemise beneath her low-cut bodice. Then she noticed a movement down the hall. She could have sworn it was Cousin John in all of his lupine glory. She followed him silently, curious as to what could take him to this part of the house. He ducked furtively into a room and then closed the door behind him.

Althea heard voices behind the door and bent down to peer through the keyhole. There were several men, unmasked, seated around a table like the kind used for cards. John took his mask off and sat down in the chair farthest from the door. He laughed at something one of the men said to him and replied, "But Verlyn has found me a capital pair, I assure you! The finest steppers you ever did see."

The man passed John a strange wrought cup saying, "Would that I had your resources, Bingham." John took a long drink and set the cup back on the table.

Only it wasn't a cup, Althea now perceived. It was a skull.

CHAPTER FIFTEEN

Althea stared at the men, trying to identify them, but it was hopeless. She had never paid enough attention to Lord John's intimates to know all of their names. She heard a rustle of silk and footsteps behind her. Someone was coming down the hall. Althea ducked into the opposite room and hid on the other side of the door. This room was dark and refreshingly cool. She sighed with relief.

The footsteps stopped, and before Althea could take another breath, a figure moved into the room, shutting the door behind him. In the light of the hall, Althea could only make out his size and the fact that he was clad in a dark domino, but once he was in the room, the darkness enveloped him. Althea stayed silent, waiting for something to happen.

He spoke in that same whisper as before, "Why so shy?"

Althea inhaled quickly, catching a whiff of that familiar cologne.

"Ah, I have frightened you. But surely you knew I would come again?"

Althea managed a faint, "No."

He moved toward the sound of her voice. "Who could stay away from such a charming insect?"

She remained silent.

"Speak to me again so that I may find you."

"That would not be wise," she replied, moving quietly away from the sound of his footsteps.

"No, but folly often brings delight, and I find that I cannot resist you after all." He moved in her direction.

"Who are you?"

"You cannot expect me to own my identity so easily."

"I know who you are."

"Although I do not doubt your intellect, I would hazard a guess that you do not."

"But why must you steal? Your position gives you money enough."

"For what do any of us live our lives?" he whispered.

"That is not an answer."

"It wasn't meant to be." Then all of a sudden, he was beside her, a strong hand gripping her elbow. "You cannot know how the thought of you has haunted me." The hand released her and slid slowly up her arm, and Althea felt a strange paralysis come over her. His other hand found her shoulder, and he brought her to him, clasping her tight. He leaned his head down and found her mouth. Kissing her softly at first, reverently, and then, when she found herself responding, with an ardor that made her very veins catch fire.

She caught her breath and pulled away enough to say, "No, this cannot be."

His lips found her throat. "I know," he murmured into her hair. "I know, but yet—"

"No yet," Althea pulled away again, this time escaping out of his reach on her light cat feet. "This was never my intention."

"Nor mine, but I too am an insect—a moth to flame."

"Look, sir, although you may hide your identity, the greatest minds of the country are following your every move."

"Yours included?"

Althea hesitated, but decided that truth was best. "Yes. You must know that you cannot continue on forever. Eventually you will be caught, and the punishment shall be severe."

"Are you frightened for me, my little insect?"

"No more frightened than you should be for yourself."

"But I am not frightened."

"Then you are a fool."

"I doubt you'll see me hang anytime soon."

Althea was about to reply when there were voices in the hall, male voices, raised in laughter. She felt a hand grasp her elbow.

The whisper dropped lower. "Quiet now. Do not pull away."

"You must let me go. I must return to the ballroom."

"And you shall, I promise. No, do not be afraid. I will endeavor to refrain from coming to you again unless I can do so as an honest man."

"I do not know how that may be," she said.

"I trust in your forgiveness."

Althea shook her head, thinking about what sort of honest proposal a lord and thief could possibly have for her. Despite what she had said to Norwich, she did not relish the thought of a liaison, however discreet the gentleman might be. "You'll need more than my forgiveness."

"Most likely. But come, the hall sounds deserted once more. You must leave first, and then I shall see to my escape."

When Althea returned to the ballroom, it was just past midnight. She slowly unhooked the mask from her headdress, aware of the curious stares from the people around her. How hypocritical was this London society where one could carry on barely disguised affaires with all manner of people and yet a simple dress branded one a hussy? She stiffened her spine and moved through the crowd, searching for the Queen of Sheba.

Instead she found the unmasked Queen of Hearts. "You are radiant, my dear," the plump lady said. "I can see why the men are all head over heels in love. Don't let the biddies intimidate you. It's all jealousy in the end."

"Oh my." Althea's heart sank. "Lady Pickney."

She executed a short curtsey and, perceiving Althea's discomfort, smiled. "I promise I shall not eat you."

"No, of course not," Althea said with a relieved smile and a curtsey of her own.

Lady Pickney took Althea's arm and wrapped it confidently around her own. "Come, dear Lady Trent, let us take a stroll around the room and show these rattles a thing or two."

The next afternoon, Althea found herself in the blue salon sipping tea with Lady Levanwood while that lady tried valiantly to resist a honey cake. Althea had worked furiously to complete her beetle manuscript and upon submission to Lord Aldridge the week prior, felt a sense of relief tempered with anxiety that Aldridge would find the manuscript wanting. The wait was excruciating, but it was better to focus on her manuscript than her hopeless entanglement with the thief. She shifted in her chair, struggling to pay attention to Lady Levanwood when her mind was in the halls of the Royal Society and fitfully in a darkened room, trapped in the arms of a masked man.

Lady Levanwood eyed a honey cake hungrily as she said to Althea, "To be sure, dear Althea, I would not have expected you to be quite so daring, for I did hear a bit of talk, you must know. And I would have warned you if I had really looked at that dress, but when one gets into conversation—well, never mind that. However, I suppose all's well that ends well. I don't know how you managed to get that Pickney woman round your finger, but since you did, I don't think I'll hear half as much chatter as I would have otherwise. She can say the foulest things with that toothy smile of hers. It puts me all out of patience. Then again, the Pickneys are such an old distinguished family and so rich that the Lord knows but they could own half of England if they wanted to. Although she's actually a Medway, but that's an old family, too."

Althea merely smiled. "I found her to be quite delightful."

"Yes I'm sure. All the men were mad for her when she came out, for she was such a delicate little thing. Pretty as a china doll. Of course, that hasn't been true for years. In fact, every year she seems to get larger and larger."

She was cut off by the sound of the door opening. Charles walked into the room with a determined step, but upon catching sight of Althea, he stopped. "Oh, cousin, I did not think to find you here."

"No, I'm afraid I turned down Sir Neville's kind invitation to take a ride in his new chaise and four. But do not let me interfere. It seems clear that you have some business to discuss with your dear mother." She rose quickly and crossed the room. "I think I will write some letters." She closed the door behind her, but instead of walking to the library, she crouched down, her eye through the keyhole.

"Mother, one would think that you would have more sense than to just sit here eating cakes."

"Really Charles, what else would you have me do?"

"But you must reason with him. He can't continue with the bank. We have lost too much and don't have time to put it to rights. Surely he would listen to you."

"Since when has he ever listened to me?" she said bitterly. "I have never been anything to him, as you are well aware. Besides, why should I worry? I'm sure it will all come out right." She took bite of cake. "It always does."

Charles growled in frustration. "Because of me! I am the one who always puts things to rights! You and John just continue as if you haven't a care in the world."

"Hush. The whole house will hear you."

Althea heard a footsteps behind her and hastily stood. She could feel the eyes of someone upon her back. She turned slowly.

CHAPTER SIXTEEN

"Cousin Althea, just the person I wished to find." A smile slid across John's face.

"Yes?" Althea replied, determined to brazen it out.

"It's about those drawings you did for me. I have need of more."

"Indeed?"

"Yes. You see, some fellows and I have got a little game going—well a challenge, more like. Of poetry. Beauty out of horror, you see."

"I don't know that I do."

"We each write a poem about some ghastly thing, but in the most beautiful language. Come to the library, and I will show you how far I've got."

Althea followed cautiously. John shut the door behind them with a click. The sound sent shivers up her spine. She told herself that she was just being silly.

John motioned her over to the large desk stationed in the corner opposite Lady Levanwood's writing desk. He picked up a sheet of closely written lines and handed it to her. The piece began:

> *The bright-winged creature lighted on the majestic purple of her skin, mottled like water drops in a placid pool.*

Althea looked up at John with raised eyebrows. "What is this?"

"Do you like it? You gave me the idea with all our talk of beetles and decay." He gestured excitedly at the paper. "Don't you see? It is a beetle feeding on a corpse, the corpse of a beautiful maiden. And here," he pointed farther down, "is the best part."

> *And like the suckling of a babe at its mother's breast, the beetle took of her essence a sweet ambrosia.*

John grinned at her.

Althea handed the paper back to John. "Quite lovely. What sort of drawings did you have in mind?"

"The corpse, of course, with the beetle just lighting on her cheek."

"In pen only, or do you desire watercolor as well?"

"Color I think, don't you?"

"If you want the full effect, then I suppose it must be color."

"Too bad there are no corpses to hand to use as a model."

Althea looked at him sharply, but he was busy examining a section of his coat sleeve through his quizzing glass.

"There seems to be a spot upon my coat." He held his arm out. "Do you not perceive it?"

Althea shook her head. She was about to ask him more about the drawings, but the idea seemed to have completely left his brain.

"Really, I think I must change. Damned nuisance. Valet should have noticed this before he handed me into it. But there is no hope for it." With that he took himself out of the room.

With everyone else otherwise occupied, Althea decided to put her free time to good use by going back through Read's notes on the Richmond Thief. Despite the presence of the thief, the Queen of Sheba had survived the masquerade ball intact. This merely confirmed Althea's suspicion that Verlyn would not stoop or did not dare to pickpocket the sapphire crown.

She walked quietly to her room and spread the bundle of notes from Mr. Read out on the tall high bed. Within an hour, she had the papers organized in stacks by crime. Eleven in all. Each crime had its own particular details, but what details did they all share? She got down off the bed and went over to the armoire. She always worked better with a visual representation of a problem, so she pulled out some writing paper and a drawing charcoal, as that is what she had to hand.

She carefully listed the details of each crime and ordered the crimes chronologically, assigning each a number based on that order. Then she studied the list. There had to be some pattern. Some detail about the crimes that would induce the moneyed and titled Verlyn to commit robbery. But the more she studied her list, the more her head hurt.

Then she had an idea. Perhaps it was the differences between the crimes that would provide the clue. She examined her list again, looking for a detail that was particular to only a few of the crimes, or maybe one.

There were two robberies where silver had been taken as well as jewelry. In the first, it had been a silver-backed hand mirror, and in the second, a candlestick. She took another piece of paper and wrote "property other than jewelry" and then noted numbers three and seven. She studied her list once more. What else about the items stolen was different? Then she had a sudden memory of her first meeting with Mr. Read. They had talked of jewelry cases as well as jewels. She examined her list again.

It was odd. Some of the crimes seemed to follow the initial theft of the Richmond earrings. They included the theft of jewels and jewel cases. In several others, including the Levanwood diamond theft, the jewels were removed and the cases left open. Perhaps the difference lay in the question of opportunity. If Verlyn found the cases locked, he took them, but if he found them open, he took only the jewels.

However, the locks on the Levanwood case had been forced, so why had Verlyn not just taken the case? And how had he gained access to the house? The easiest thing would have been to attend the party as a guest, but he hadn't let society know that he was in town. But again, why would the son of a duke have a need to steal the jewels of others? The Norwich family was known to be rich. Unless they hid their debts like the Levanwoods did?

And what about Cousin John? His behavior had become increasingly troublesome. Was he connected with the missing valet and the maid Mary? And how to explain his renewed ability to acquire yet another pair of expensive horses? Could he be tied somehow to the theft of the Levanwood diamonds? John knew Verlyn and had expressed disdain of his mother's jewelry. Perhaps there was some point of connection between them. The horses could be a payment for John's collusion in Verlyn's criminal operation.

A faint tap on the door startled Althea out of her reverie. She hastily gathered the papers and the charcoal together and then, barring a better hiding place, shoved them under the bed.

Bridgett entered with a pitcher of warm water. "What gown would milady like for this evening?" And catching sight of Althea's blackened hands, "Oh dear, what happened to your ladyship?"

"I'm just organizing my charcoals. Lord John asked me to do some sketches for him, and I find my charcoal box is all in disarray. Forgive me, for I fear you will have to fetch the water twice." Althea stuck her hands in the bowl and allowed Bridgett to pour the warm water over them, leaving a gray pool.

"'Tis nothing," Bridgett replied. "But let me lay out your ladyship's gown." She handed Althea a soft cloth to dry her hands and then went to the wardrobe with an air of expectation.

"The blue satin, I think," Althea said. "Is Lord John expected to dine with us this evening?"

"Can't say as I know." Bridgett gathered up the blue satin evening frock and laid it carefully on the bed. "He often goes out, I believe, to eat at his clubs."

"Yes. I suppose that is to be expected with a young man of fashion. To which clubs does he belong, I wonder?"

Bridgett merely shook her head. "I wouldn't know."

"No, of course not. Then again, there must be some gentleman's club particularly aligned with poetry."

"Let me fetch another pitcher of water." Bridgett bustled out the door.

Althea stood a moment, lost in thought. There had to be a way to learn just what John was up to, but how she might follow him without suspicion was beyond her. Although, if he did not appear at dinner, it was likely he would be away from the house for some time. If that were the case, it might give her a chance to search his rooms. The thought of being caught in his rooms at night was not particularly pleasing, but she would just have to think of something when the time came.

John did not make an appearance at dinner, which was a pity because the invited guests were a set of very dull people culled from Althea wasn't sure where. They were the sort of persons whose titles gave them consequence without giving them interest, and Althea was almost thankful when Charles planted himself beside her after the gentlemen had partaken of their port.

"I fear you are out of spirits," he said.

"No indeed, why do you say that?"

He smiled. "Just a certain melancholy air you have about you."

"I will try to smile more, for my spirits are not low, I can assure you."

"Good. I would hate to think that we are such poor company that you long for other."

Althea sat a little straighter. "You tease me, cousin."

He lowered his voice. "I own I find it hard to resist. But then again, when one's heart is broken, some license must be granted."

"Far be it from me to cause anyone pain, but you know my reasons. Please do not press me on this subject further."

"Surely you cannot hold out hope in that quarter. It is really too much. And after that masquerade dress, too. Trust me when I tell you that Norwich will not make you the kind of offer you should accept."

Althea gave him a hard look. "Rest assured that I am not expecting anything from the Duke of Norwich, Charles. I am perfectly content to maintain my widowed state."

He shook his head and then looked at her steadily, a strange expression in his eyes. "Perhaps. Or perhaps I have mistaken your intent."

Althea had a sudden memory of the thief's arms around her. A blush crept up her cheeks, and she turned away.

Fortunately, at that moment, Jane appeared and claimed her for piquet. Althea was thus able to avoid Charles for the rest of the evening, although she had the uneasy feeling that his eyes were upon her at every moment.

That night, after every guest had bid adieu and all of the family had climbed the stairs to their chambers, Althea sat in her wrapper in the chair by the window, wide awake. It had to be several hours past midnight, and yet she had heard no sounds of movement up the stairs. Cousin John must still be out. At least she hoped so.

Althea screwed up her courage and slowly opened the door to her room. She closed it quietly behind her, making sure to leave a crack of space in case she had to push into the room unexpectedly. She cradled the flame of the candle with her other hand, tempering the light, and crept down the hall.

John's apartments were some distance from her own, so she paused several times at faint yet startling sounds. Finally, she reached his chamber and slid in through a partially open door. She had heard enough of the servants' chatter to know that John's valet slept in an antechamber connected to the main room. She held up her candle. Good, the door to the antechamber appeared to be fully closed.

Now, where would John hide clues to his strange behavior? Or perhaps even to murder? She crossed to the large wardrobe. Surely this would be the spot where a clever man might seek to disguise his true self? She opened the heavy oak doors and then held her candle high. What a large number of clothes John possessed. There were shirts and waistcoats, cravats and she knew not what else besides. She ran her hand along the fabric of what appeared to be a silk waistcoat, suddenly very aware of how wrong her conduct must appear should anyone discover her. She pulled her hand away and then focused on the center section of the piece, which was lined with drawers.

She pulled out one drawer after the other, looking for anything of interest. Bills for a pair of boots, underclothes, a high-crowned beaver hat, gambling pledges, linen handkerchiefs, fobs and seals for a watch chain. There appeared to be nothing out of the ordinary, no sign even of eccentricity. She pulled a large drawer out and discovered a velvet bag. Perhaps this would amount to something. She set the candle on the floor and carefully opened the top of the bag.

She extracted a smooth white object and then almost dropped it in shock before she realized that the hollowed out skull she now held in her hand was nothing more than a cleverly wrought piece of glazed pottery, obviously created to drink out of. Althea studied the skull for a moment and then slipped it back in the bag and carefully slid the drawer back into place.

After a quick check to make sure that John's quarters contained complete and undamaged bellpulls, Althea quietly approached the door and put her ear to it. Silence reigned. She opened the door cautiously and stepped into the hall, careful not to let the rush of air blow her candle out. She had a strange feeling that somewhere deep within the shadowed recesses, someone watched her. She held her candle higher, seeking out the dim patches beyond the glow of flame, but could see nothing to alarm her.

I'm just being silly again, she thought, and then she carefully made her way toward her own chamber, alert to any noise. But no sound was heard along the narrow passage. The feeling of eyes upon her continued unabated, however, and when she reached her door, she turned back. She saw a shadow shift in the dark recesses of the hall and held her candle so as to see farther down the passage. But there was nothing she could see. Unwilling to retrace her steps and investigate, she moved quickly into her room and shut the door. She put her ear to the keyhole, but the only sound she perceived was the beat of her racing heart.

CHAPTER SEVENTEEN

Althea slipped out early to check on her bird, but then retreated to her room. She went down to the breakfast parlor later than usual, missing Charles but meeting John, who appeared to have arrived right before her. He seemed none the worse for his late night and in fact greeted her with a hearty, "Good morning."

"Good morning to you, cousin," she replied and placed a slice of toast on her plate. As she sat down, she studied his face. If indeed he drank, she could detect no sign of it in the healthful glow of his cheeks. "Do you think we shall have good weather today? I have a mind to do some shopping. My gloves are sadly worn from so much frivolity."

He smiled. "I should hope so, for Lady Jersey would never countenance worn gloves at one of her functions."

"Just as I feared," Althea replied. "And where would you have me go for such a thing? I wish to have gloves that might last the rest of the season."

Without even a moment of hesitation he replied, "Southerland's. They have the finest gloves in all of London."

"Thank you for such sound advice. I hope I shall have the pleasure of seeing you this evening."

"I think I shall attend. One never knows, however, just where the will of one's friends will take one."

"I see you place a great deal of emphasis on your friendships."

"Quite. They can be so valuable for so many reasons."

Later that morning, Althea cornered Jane in the blue salon. "Come dear, we must make haste. Cousin John is just now asking for his horses to be brought up from the stables."

"And why should that concern us?"

"To follow him, of course, but we must be sly. I shall make some excuse for not using our carriage and have a hackney called on the pretext of going out to buy gloves. Then we shall simply see where John goes."

So it was that a hackney coach with two ladies safely tucked inside it ground its way through the mess of London traffic in pursuit of a smart black phaeton. When the phaeton approached Pall Mall, Jane said, "Oh dear heaven, he is headed for his club! Althea, pray turn the coach around."

"Nonsense, no one need see us if we don't alight."

The phaeton approached the famous bow window of White's, and Jane huddled farther into the carriage. The hackney driver pulled in down the street and came to a stop.

"Are we just to wait here?" Jane said.

"I have a suspicion that John won't be long at White's."

"Why do you say that? This hackney won't wait forever, stopped among all of these gentlemen's carriages. Really,

Althea, I should have known you would lead me into trouble."

"Hush Jane. I've promised to pay the hackney well, so he'll do just what I say."

They waited another ten minutes, and then Althea exclaimed, "Look, there he is."

Jane straightened up from where she was crouched down. "Why, it is Cousin John. But what can he mean walking along the thoroughfare?"

"We shall find out." Althea tapped the roof of the carriage with her parasol, and the equipage lurched forward in the delicate task of maneuvering out into traffic.

John continued to walk for several blocks until he hailed a hackney coach and got in.

"Just as I suspected. The bird shall come home to roost at last," Althea said.

John's hackney kept going and going, taking a circuitous route that eventually ended up in a neat, although not fashionable, neighborhood. Althea tapped the roof of the carriage once more and their coach came to rest some distance down the quiet street. The ladies watched John alight and send his hackney away. He entered the house with a firm step.

"And now?" Jane said. "We've tracked him down to his bit of fancy."

"Why would a man go to such trouble merely to hide a mistress? You and I both know that such a thing is common enough—not Sir Arthur, to my knowledge, but certainly many otherwise respectable gentlemen. My father was called out any number of times to attend to some of the most embarrassing ailments—"

"Yes, I'm sure," Jane replied quickly.

"We must find out what goes on in that house," Althea said.

"Come Althea, we cannot simply walk up and apply the knocker. Nor can we enter the house like common thieves."

"Not in broad daylight," Althea replied.

"Not ever. Do be sensible."

"You are right." Althea stuck her head out of the window and told the driver to take them to Southerland's, but noted the location of the house as she did so.

When she returned to Levanwood House, she was met with the news that a note had been delivered for her. She thanked the footman and took the white envelope from the footman's silver tray, hurrying to the library to peruse what she was sure was a new set of instructions from Norwich. Really, there was no getting away from Norwich's plans for capture of the thief. If only Althea could convey to him the direction of her suspicions. Unfortunately, she did not know how to make him understand without confessing her own shameful part. But it must be done.

The envelope didn't come from Norwich, however. Instead, when Althea broke the black sealing wax, she found the very proper scrawl of Lord Aldridge. Her heart jumped to her throat in panic, but as her eyes scanned the words, a smile spread across her face. Her manuscript had been accepted for publication in the next *Philosophical Transactions*! It was too wonderful to be believed!

Althea raced from the library in search of Jane. That lady had taken refuge in her room and was curled in a chair with a book, but when she saw Althea, she dropped the book. "My dear Althea, what is it?"

"Only the best most exciting thing that has ever happened. My manuscript has been accepted! Oh Jane, how shall I bear so much happiness?"

Jane got up and put her arms around Althea. "My dearest sister, I'm sure you shall soon become accustomed to the receipt of accolades."

That evening, still unable to stop a smile from continuously spreading across her face, Althea arrayed herself in a new dress of sea-blue silk adorned simply with gold braiding at the waist, her new kid gloves, and a pair of striped satin slippers that she had also seen at Southerland's and couldn't resist. Her hair was done in her usual severe style, with thick bands of gold braid woven together instead of the lace cap habitually worn by other dowager ladies.

Jane had chosen blue as well, and so when Sir Neville approached them soon after their arrival at Lady Jersey's palatial house, he said, "Behold, two nymphs sprung from the cerulean waters of the ocean."

Jane looked embarrassed, but Althea laughed. "Very pretty, Sir Neville. I assure you we did not put our minds together this evening to coordinate our dresses. And once we were down, it was too late to change again."

He gallantly offered an arm to each lady saying, "Do not talk of change, when I shall be the envy of all the gentlemen here."

"Indeed you are," said Lord Casterleigh, turning away from a group of gentlemen to greet Althea and Jane. He entered the ballroom with them and then solicited Althea for the country dance that was just forming. As the season had progressed, they had formed an easy relationship that might have been called friendship had their roles been different.

However the baron might enjoy her company, he had not so far behaved in a manner that would have changed their status. Perhaps his youth made him wary of attachment, or he feared his cousin Norwich's supposed wrath should his attentions grow too particular.

As they took their places, Casterleigh said, "I see that I am not in favor with your cousin."

"Indeed?" She looked around, for both John and Charles had accompanied the Levanwood party.

"You can be in no doubt of which cousin I mean. Carlton seemed about to call me out when I stole a march on him and claimed this dance."

"Cousin Charles knows my heart is not easily touched, particularly by such dramatic scenes."

"Yes, the *frozen widow*." Casterleigh laughed. "That is what they call you."

"*They* being the men who place bets on such things in their clubs?"

"In all propriety I should deny it, but your frankness of manner prevents me."

"And why *frozen*? Surely my frankness of manner gives the opposite impression."

"It does, but I believe the fact that you have not apparently succumbed to any earnest declarations marks you as a cold heart. It is even said that you sent poor Verlyn abroad again."

"He has left England? So suddenly?"

"You did not know? That must put a lie to the rumors."

"They had no foundation, I can assure you." However, some part of Althea had to acknowledge that she wouldn't have been entirely unhappy if they had.

When the dance ended, she was forced to dance the second with Charles, but this passed in hard silence, neither willing to begin conversation. Upon the conclusion of the dance, they were met by a surprise guest.

"Squire Pettigrew!" Althea said, and then recovering her powers of tact, "How delightful to see you."

"And I you, dear Lady Trent. Although I do in general prefer quieter evenings, a ball such as this, given by a lady of Lady Jersey's exalted reputation, cannot be missed. In fact, as you will no doubt notice, I have even fitted myself out for the occasion with new evening attire. But just so that there can be no misunderstanding of the matter, I am not enamored of such high shirt points." He turned his head stiffly as if to demonstrate. "Unfortunately, I find that no tailor will consent to lower them. What strange fashions these London swells have, isn't that right, Lady Trent?"

His tone implied such a level of familiarity that it made Althea cringe, but she soldiered on. "Each society has its own fashions. You have met my cousin, Lord Charles, I believe?"

"Sir, it is a very great pleasure to finally make your acquaintance. The marchioness has been so kind as to receive my calls any number of times. I'm afraid you have been absent, but we have made quite a lively party nonetheless."

"Sir," Charles replied with all the hauteur he was capable of.

Pettigrew seemed immune to the snub and continued to chat animatedly until Althea had the good thought to send him for refreshment. When he was barely out of earshot, Charles exclaimed, "I don't know what Sally Jersey was thinking to invite such an encroaching mushroom!"

Althea would normally have agreed, especially since she had hoped that an unknown country squire would escape the notice of the society hostesses and thus leave her evenings Pettigrew-less. However, she felt a certain indignation at Charles's lofty tone. More to spite Charles than to defend Pettigrew, she said, "The squire is a very good man who has been my neighbor for many years. You may dislike his pretensions, but I would have you take care not to disparage him in my presence!"

Charles lip curled. "Forgive me, madam. I have maligned your favorite."

Althea glared at him and, catching sight of Pettigrew coming toward them, gave Pettigrew an encouraging smile. That gentleman reached them ere long saying, "Indeed, I had not thought to meet with such a great number of acquaintances. It is quite delightful to be so well known in London."

At that fatuous remark, Charles left Althea to deal with Pettigrew as she would. Fortunately for Althea's well-being, she was still bathed in the contented afterglow of her triumph with the Royal Society. And Jane and Sir Neville appeared just as thoughts of beetles could not maintain Althea's equilibrium. The group talked of London and Dettamoor Park for the span of several dances. Then Sir Neville succumbed to the temptation of a reel, and Jane agreed, leaving Althea once again in the squire's clutches. He declined the reel in favor of further conversation.

As Althea listened with half an ear to a tedious description of all the surprising things Pettigrew had learned about London in his brief sojourn in the capital, she scanned the crowd for any acquaintance who might save her from further boredom. None appeared, and she had just given herself up for lost when she noticed Norwich moving toward her. She caught his eye and smiled. He responded in kind, and she realized that he knew just what was passing through her mind. When had their brains become so attuned?

"Ah, Lady Trent, I believe we are of a like mind," Pettigrew continued. "Let me take this opportunity to tell you how happy you have made me."

"Pardon?" Althea snapped back to attention. Now what was Pettigrew saying? He must have taken her smile for assent. But before she could ask for clarification, Norwich reached them.

"My dance, I believe, Lady Trent." He extended his hand.

"Let us continue our conversation at another moment," Althea said to Pettigrew as she put her hand in Norwich's. And when Pettigrew was out of earshot she added, "Thank you, sir. You have saved me from one of the most tedious conversations I have had to endure yet this evening."

Norwich merely nodded.

"Have I said something amiss?" Althea continued. "For surely my remark was made for commentary—either upon Squire Pettigrew's discourse or my acid tongue."

"You would do well to avoid that man's company."

"For my own pleasure, I would heartily agree, except that one cannot snub one's nearest neighbors, even when their conversation leaves much to be desired."

They took their places, and Norwich replied, "Rattles like that may do no end of evil in the name of conversation."

They took a turn, and Althea said, "In a restricted neighborhood that may be true, but one would hope that London society would think twice before believing a country squire in matters of importance."

"I am always amazed at what London may believe. One cannot escape the past, unfortunately."

He seemed unusually taciturn after that remark, so, still occupied with Royal Society musings, Althea left him to his thoughts. They parted soon after, and he did not approach her again, although she felt his eyes upon her once or twice. Unfortunately, Pettigrew took his place and remain possessively at her side for the rest of the evening.

CHAPTER EIGHTEEN

The next morning, Althea arose early, checked on the raven that wasn't more than a skeleton now, and re-entered the house by slipping into the kitchen. Her morning walks had not gone unnoticed by the staff, but so far nothing had been said to Lady Levanwood. Mr. Mauston was awake as usual, preparing the food that would soon be served in the breakfast parlor. Althea usually passed through, but this morning she had to be sure of her quarry before she set out on a fool's errand.

"Mr. Mauston, have you seen whether Lord Bingham returned last night? He was not in the carriage, but I know that he often returns later, and I wished to have private speech with him this morning."

"My understanding is that Lord Bingham returned sometime after three o'clock, but has yet to leave his room. At least, he hasn't called for his tea, madam."

"One can hardly expect him to after such a late evening. Thank you."

She moved quickly up the back staircase and then down the hall to her room. She pulled a black gown from where she had hidden it away and then rang the bellpull. When a maid appeared, she asked for Sally, and when that young lady finally appeared, Althea put her hand over her mouth in a gesture of silence. "I'll need help with one of my black dresses again."

Sally nodded in understanding, and Althea continued in a low voice. "I will need you to summon me a hackney coach if such a thing can be procured at this hour. With the utmost discretion, you understand, for I shall endeavor to return to the house unnoticed after I have completed my errand."

After she was properly arrayed in her bombazine dress and a large, rather unfashionable bonnet with a heavy swath of netting completely obscuring her face, Althea sent Sally downstairs with the coins she would need to interest one of the urchins, forever loitering about the London streets, in hailing a hackney carriage on her behalf. As Althea entered the carriage, she gave the driver the address and then sat back so that she would not be observed as the hack maneuvered through streets already alive with the morning's commerce. She felt she had most of the story, as disjointed as it was, but several important points eluded certainty. She would have to be careful.

When the carriage stopped, Althea asked the driver to wait. The church bells had just struck nine o'clock—not a fashionable hour to be calling, but Althea didn't have much choice. She alighted from the carriage and walked up the stone steps to the wooden door. Several raps of the knocker brought a shy lady's maid who indicated her mistress was not yet up but let Althea enter upon production of one of Althea's gilt-edged calling cards.

An hour and a half later, Althea entered the carriage well satisfied with her morning's work. She directed the hack toward Bow Street in hopes of finding Mr. Read before the press of cases made speaking with him impossible.

It would be hard to describe a greater contrast between the silence of their previous meeting and the disorder of the magistrate's court. Bailiffs jostled with spectators and the accused, many bedraggled and thin. Voices shouted over each other, punctuated at random by the rapping of Magistrate Read's gavel upon the oak of his table. Althea watched, half in fascination and half in amusement, as Read attempted to impose the order required to listen to the pleadings of an accused who appeared to still be under the influence of the previous night's revels.

It took a moment for the crowd to assimilate the presence of a lady in deepest mourning, who, although not dressed at the height of fashion, was certainly a gentlewoman. The crowd closest to the door moved aside, parting like the Red Sea. This was a welcome reaction. Althea had supposed that the open court of Bow Street, like its surrounding neighborhood, might not be the safest place for a lady and had brought a stout parasol for self-defense.

One of the bailiffs hurried over, pushing the curious even farther from her. "Begging your pardon, madam, I think you must be mistaken. This is not a fit place for such as you."

"None fitter. I must speak with Magistrate Read, if you would please conduct me to his private chambers."

"But madam, he has many cases yet to hear this morning."

"Never mind, I shall be happy to wait." With that she pushed forward in the direction of Read's chambers.

The commotion at the back of the room finally caught Read's attention. He banged the gavel down. "Let the lady pass. Bailiff, escort her to chambers so she may wait in peace."

Once Althea had reached the stuffy back room, the bailiff helped her clear a space on one of the rickety chairs, and she sat to await an audience. After an hour of study of every dead insect collected on the window ledge, some that she recognized from her last visit and some newly acquired, Read finally flew into the room, all rumpled energy. "Lady Trent, how sorry I am that you had to wait."

"No need to apologize, Mr. Read. It is I who am intruding upon you. And I must beg your pardon for not returning your notes to you this morning. I had meant to, but left in such a hurry that it escaped my mind."

"Think nothing of it. May I assume that you have found them helpful?"

"Yes, although I am not sure to what end. Upon review of the individual crimes, I noticed that in some cases the thief stole only the jewelry and in some cases the box as well."

"Does it mean something?"

"I don't know, but this difference bothers me. And some crimes appear to be more like the work of a clever pickpocket—one that preys upon high society in situ, so to speak. If one focuses only on those crimes, one might think the thief is a servant, hired on as extra help for balls."

"I considered the possibility, but, as I think I mentioned at our first meeting, the crimes seem too similar to be the work of more than one man, and one servant would not likely have access to so many houses."

"True, even if the servant were a woman and had access to a lady's boudoir," Althea added, hoping that her face didn't betray the lie. "I'm not sure where this can all lead, but I felt it necessary to give you my thoughts in case they may be of assistance."

They talked for several minutes more about Althea's general theories, and then she asked him if he had made any connection between particular jewelers and the thefts. "For I have thought that perhaps the thief merely fences the jewels to some unscrupulous jeweler who then smuggles them abroad."

Mr. Read indicated that some of the stolen jewelry had been recently refurbished at a jeweler named Portnoy, but then added, "As Mr. Portnoy's establishment is frequented by the fashionable, that is hardly surprising."

"I had noted that detail. Howe and Cartwright did good business as well. I shall have to go back and review the notes again. And Mr. Read, I also came to advise you of a most important turn of events. The Royal Society shall be publishing a monograph that I feel certain you would like to review." Althea explained briefly about her conversation with Lord Aldridge and gave Read an outline of her manuscript thesis.

"Delightful, Lady Trent. You have described a process of real use to Bow Street. I anxiously await a copy of your manuscript." Then he apologized that he did not have more time to discuss the monograph and excused himself to attend to his court.

The bailiff returned and escorted Althea safely to the waiting carriage. It was just coming on midday when Althea arrived at Levanwood House. She fled up the back stairs to her room. If the two servants she passed on the staircase thought her costume odd, they didn't presume to say so. She was safe yet again.

Unfortunately, her peace was short-lived. Bridgett had just helped her into a more modish day dress when Jane bustled in.

"You have no idea the uproar this morning! And where were you? I did not see you at breakfast."

Althea indicated that Bridgett was free to go and then turned to Jane. "You know very well where I went."

"Not to spy on John?"

"Not spying, merely investigating a few salient points—like the identity of the occupant of the house. But do give me your news first."

"There was a row this morning, right at the breakfast table, between Charles and John. Shouting so loud that the whole house could hear it."

"What about?"

"John's carriage, of all things. Charles indicated that it was a waste of money and so showy that it couldn't possibly be trusted to carry him anywhere but in London."

"Seems an odd argument to have at the breakfast table. Perhaps the bills from the coach maker have become more pressing. Or perhaps John did buy those horses after all."

"That's what I thought. This is a strange house, Althea."

"I fear it may prove stranger still. I have been thinking that it would be beneficial to return to Dettamoor Park. The Levanwoods unnerve me in a way that I can't quite explain."

Jane sighed. "And I had such high hopes to bring you back as a bride, but I suppose that if there is no man who suits you—"

Althea had a sudden recollection of the thief's arms around her and quickly banished the thought. "And you, dear Jane? If Sir Neville does not come up to snuff soon, I shall box his ears!"

Jane sighed again and flung herself into a chair. "He has. I am the problem."

Althea sat down opposite her. "So I have not been mistaken in him. Pray tell me everything."

"I think I am too old for marriage. That is the only reason I can explain to myself why I have not already accepted his obliging proposal."

"Perhaps you do not love him—although, as we both know, love is not a prerequisite for a happy union."

"I esteem him. He is silly like all men of his stamp, but kind and devoted. He told me that I was the only woman he could ever love, but he had given up all hope when I retired from society."

"A very proper sentiment for a man who wants to marry you. Do you think you would be happy as Lady Tabard?"

"I do not know, and that is what concerns me. Then again, I am past the age of blushing passion, so I suppose my hesitation is merely fear of the unknown. I have had such freedom at Dettamoor Park."

"Sir Neville does not strike me as the sort of man to constrain you much. And please do not take it into your head to make decisions out of concern for me. I love you, dear sister, and would not confine you in any way. I would be the first to wish you joy."

"I know. It is the uncertainty of my own happiness. I shall have to give it time and thought."

"That is the right course. For as much as the poets prattle on about passion, love tends to creep upon one, like the intertwining threads of the ivy up the bricks of a wall."

Jane smiled. "You are still young, Althea. Don't settle for the ivy when you might yet have the flame."

Althea laughed to hide her discomfort. She had been playing with fire too long and must put her heart back on the rational path.

It was in a spirit of resignation, therefore, that she prepared herself for a small party at the Ravenscrest's house. Such parties could boast of nothing more exciting than supper, cards, and perhaps some halfhearted dancing to the rhythmless plinking of the piano keys by any spinster the family could produce. However, there was always the hope that Lord Ravenscrest had invited men of his own scientific stamp. Althea took heart in that possibility.

She dressed with her usual care in a cream silk gown with a red figured design. Her hair was smooth and simple, and she wore a small cap fixed to her glossy tresses. A garnet brooch and earrings, which were given to her by her father, finished the toilette. When Bridgett was done with her ministrations, Althea went down to the blue salon to wait for the Levanwood party.

She found Charles there, already dressed and in unusually good humor. "Ah, fair cousin, how lovely you look this evening."

"Thank you, Charles. I think this evening should be enjoyable, don't you?"

He smiled. "Tolerable. The Ravenscrests can be counted on for a well-prepared meal. Their chef is French. But as to the conversation, I wouldn't hold out too much hope."

"At least you shall have the men's part of it. You have no idea how insipid the ladies talk can be. It is nothing but gossip from end to end."

Charles laughed, and at that moment the door opened to admit Jane and Lord Levanwood. The family group chatted about nothing in particular until Lady Levanwood made her entrance in a dark rose satin gown and a feathered turban of the same material. Althea could not help but notice that the turban made her head look misshapen, but she refrained from commenting.

As they were about to ascend into the Levanwood's carriage, Althea turned to Jane. "Where is Cousin John? Will he not be accompanying us?"

"No," Jane replied in a low voice. "Lady Levanwood is quite put out. John went for a ride in that phaeton of his this morning and has not returned."

"I bet he went to prove Charles wrong with some trip into the country."

"Very likely," Jane agreed.

The Ravenscrests had gathered a group of persons more likely culled from young Lady Ravenscrest's acquaintance than the more scientifically minded men of Lord Ravenscrest's set, and Althea struggled through vapid conversation with a young man of significantly more style than wit. It was almost a relief to retire with the ladies and to the world of domestic concerns, gossip, and fashion.

The men soon joined them, however. The coffee and tea emerged, and Charles came over to Althea to ask if she desired refreshment.

"Coffee, thank you," Althea replied, grateful that his pleasant manners still held firm.

By the time Charles returned, Lord Ravenscrest had sought Althea out for further discussion of her paper for the *Philosophical Transactions* and for that purpose had stationed himself beside her on a settee meant for two.

"It represents some of Sir Arthur's most exciting research," Althea said as Charles handed her the cup. "A novel application of his previous investigations. Thank you, Charles."

Charles nodded and with a half smile upon his lips said, "From everything I have ever heard, Sir Arthur Trent was a paragon of scientific virtue."

Althea sipped her coffee. It was not particularly good coffee, and she put the cup back on the saucer, wishing she had asked for tea. "He was quite ahead of his time."

"And when shall we have the privilege of reading this manuscript?" Ravenscrest said.

"I have been told that it should be part of the next *Philosophical Transactions* and, if the Society deems it proper, I might even have the privilege of presenting the principal findings at a meeting."

"But surely you would find such a presentation taxing? I would be happy to perform the duty for you."

Althea took another sip of the bitter coffee so that she wouldn't betray her annoyance at this obvious ploy. "That is most kind, Lord Ravenscrest, but I feel I owe it to my late husband to perform the task. I know he would have wanted it that way."

"My cousin is a most devoted widow," Charles added with a hint of mirth.

Althea looked at him sharply. "I know my duty."

"Of course," Ravenscrest said quickly. "I'm sure that is most proper, but you may count on me at any time."

"Thank you, I shall keep that in mind."

Then there occurred a rather awkward silence that Althea dealt with by swallowing more of the vile coffee. She was rescued by Lady Ravenscrest, who came to encourage her husband to join others in a game of cards. She also sent Charles about his business, relegating him to another table with a set of persons invited solely for obligation. Althea could read Charles's discontent from across the room.

Althea fared better with a couple of dowagers and Jane. The ladies may have been old, but they were smarter than their young descendants and more willing to speak in a frank way that Althea couldn't help but admire. Whist with such a group was quite pleasant. They whiled away their time until the carriages could be called to carry them all back to Levanwood House.

It was only when Althea prepared for bed that she started to feel strange. She sent Bridgett away and sat down with her wrapper pulled firmly across her nightdress. Her head began to swim something awful. She put it down on her lap, but that did not seem to help. She felt the darkness pulling at her brain, sucking her down in a black abyss of unconsciousness. Then her body was pulled along as she slipped quietly from the chair onto the floor.

CHAPTER NINETEEN

Althea awoke to the scratch of a pen on paper. Her head felt leaden and her mouth dry. She opened her eyes slowly, becoming accustomed to the fetid light seeping through the waxed paper affixed to a square window. The room smelled of sweat and bile. A figure sat hunched at a small table in front of the window.

"Charles?" she said wonderingly, not sure if her eyes deceived her. It was that coffee he had given her!

The pen stopped, and he turned ever so slightly. "Yes, my dear?"

She tried to move, but she realized that she was still in her nightgown and wrapper, bound with a length of rope to the chair on which she sat, her arms pulled painfully behind the back of the chair and wrists tied together. "Charles, what is this?"

He smiled a slow, menacing smile. "Nothing but a little persuasion, my beloved wife."

"Wife?" A shiver ran down her spine. "But I remember no marriage."

"A mere formality, but how pleased I am that you desire the consummation of our union as much as I do."

She took a deep breath to steady her nerves. What had her father always said? Panic never saved anyone. "I believe you are mistaken. As much as I admire you, cousin, my heart would never allow me to take such a step."

He laughed. "Your heart? What has that organ got to do with anything? Really, Althea, you are doing it a bit too brown. Your heart clearly did not prevent you giving Pettigrew the yes you have denied me."

"Pettigrew? But I didn't agree to marry him. How can you think I would?"

"Of course you did. He persuaded half the ton that he came to an understanding with you back in Somerset. Besides, I overheard the fool propose to you again at Sally Jersey's ball. Instead of sending the fellow to the right about, you encouraged his advances."

"I did not! It was all a misunderstanding. Charles, you must believe me. I am still of the same mind about marriage."

"Forgive me, then, for believing you capable of anything to spite me, but it is of no matter. Pettigrew may say what he likes when we are married."

"But I will not marry you, cousin."

"Your desire is immaterial. I need you to marry me and so you shall, whether you like to or not."

"It was always my money?"

"And your lovely person. But when one is facing debtor's prison, one cannot be too particular."

"Surely things aren't as bad as all that?" she said in a rallying tone.

"Very much so. Between that cretin of a brother and my hen-witted mother, we have had to mortgage almost everything. And that leaves me without a feather to fly with, my dear. The blood-sucking moneylenders will have their due."

"Your father has no power to prevent the family's ruin?"

"My father has done what he can. Unfortunately, our debts are beyond my father's skill at faro to repair. We have run out of time."

"So you faked the disappearance of the diamonds to fund the faro bank? There is no Richmond Thief?"

"Very clever of you. But whether there is a thief or no, I care not. It was merely an excuse my father used to collect from Lloyds and sell the stones. The old man is smarter than I had given him credit for. But even he didn't count on John and mother doubling their already excessive spending. When I heard about those damn horses John meant to buy on top of everything else, I knew more drastic measures had to be taken."

"But Charles, there must be other young women of fortune willing to ally with such a noble family. You cannot tell me that an eligible bachelor must go without a wife."

He laughed again. "What a simpleton you are. If it were merely money, then I suppose we could come about. But the Levanwoods have never smelt of the shop. It does not befit us. And suitable women do not fall all over themselves to catch a younger son."

"But John?"

"He will never marry."

"How can you be so sure?"

Charles's eyes turned cold. "Because one cannot marry a corpse, my love. I sent him on a little carriage ride from which he shall not return."

"You sabotaged his carriage?"

"He should be in a ditch by now, his neck broken in two. And if that doesn't do it, some obliging footpads will finish him off for me."

Althea sucked in her breath. It was all making sense now—the disappearances of the Levanwood servants and the missing valet.

Charles returned to his paper and continued writing. Then he paused and turned back to her. "No more questions? Or perhaps you are afraid to ask. Do not worry. There shall be plenty of time to talk, a lifetime in fact. Although, if you do not please me, yours may be shorter than you had anticipated." He focused on his paper, dusting it with sand and then gently sealing the whole with red sealing wax.

"Where are we?" Althea said when she had regained her courage.

"Somewhere out of the way. They will think we are on the Great North Road, and so we shall be in a couple of days when no one is looking for us. Until then, we shall remain here in London, biding our time. It's a pity you are a widow. A maid would be so much simpler." He looked beyond her, and she followed his gaze to a rickety bed pushed up against the wall.

"We are to be married over the anvil in Gretna Green?" Althea said as calmly as she could.

"Yes. You can see why I do not risk the banns, and in our present state, I think I shall forgo the cost of a special license."

"I suppose."

He stood up and walked over to her. He reached his hand out and slowly caressed her cheek. "Dear Althea, how lovely you look when you are angry." His hand traveled down to her throat and then rested there suggestively. "I like a woman of spirit." His thumb pressed inward, and Althea felt her airway closing. "Particularly when I tame her."

Althea coughed and sputtered, rocking the chair back and forth, trying desperately to loosen his grip. Then suddenly he let go. "Lovely, my dear, truly lovely. I think I will become quite accustomed to the chains of matrimony."

He picked up the paper from the desk and donned his caped driving coat. "I shall be gone several hours." He planted a kiss on her head. "Try not to miss me too much."

She heard the door close behind her and the sound of a key turning in the lock. As soon as his footsteps died away, she willed her mind to take stock of the room and encounter a plan of escape. The paper window would be no match if she hurled herself through it, but she could not tell how high up the room might be. Unless there was something to break her fall, a leap from the window might be fatal.

And there was the matter of the rope. She twisted her wrists, but she only managed to cut them as the rope held tight. After several minutes of struggle, she noticed that the candle Charles had used to warm the wax seal was still burning. Perhaps, if she could make her way to the table, she could burn the rope off without killing herself in the process, although the rumpled bed in the corner made her think that death might be a preferable fate to being Charles's wife.

Her legs were free, thank goodness, so she rocked the chair forward and fell upon her knees. Slowly, very slowly, she inched her way forward, holding the weight of the chair upon her back. Once at the table, she pushed herself to stand, still bent over with the chair. Feeling for the candle with her fingers, she pulled her wrists toward the flame.

It took all of her willpower not to cry out from the pain as the flame wicked up the rope and took hold. She gritted her teeth, and then, when she thought that she could not stand it any longer, she yanked hard and the rope gave way, sending pieces of the burning cord down onto the floor. Althea frantically stamped them out, her movement ungainly under the weight of the chair. With much effort, she set the chair back onto the floor. She pulled her hands from behind her and inspected the damage. Her skin was red, and she could see where it had started to pucker into blisters, but she ignored the pain and loosed the rope where it bound her to the chair.

She stood, shaken and stiff. Her head swam, but she took a deep breath and steadied her nerves. She had to figure out how to escape. She went to the window and pushed at the paper. It was old and brittle and gave way easily to her fingernail. She ripped it out and flung the pieces to the floor. The room appeared to be located on the second story of a ramshackle building above a refuse-strewn street. It faced a dark alleyway that stank with the waste of the gutter. Two stories was a shorter distance than she had dared hope, but still a fall from this height was likely to cause injury. Then she would truly be at Charles's mercy.

Althea looked down and saw the carcass of a spider, dead upon the windowsill. Poor creature. Suddenly, she had a vision of a spider repelling down from her silken web. "I shall be that spider," she thought. She gathered up the charred ends of the ropes that had bound her. Perhaps, if they were all knotted together, they might form a long enough rope to at least get her within several feet of the ground. With renewed vigor, Althea forced her sore hands to work, knotting the thick rope as tightly as possible. Together the pieces made a cord some ten feet in length.

With her heart thumping loudly in her ears, she looped the rope around a leg of the table and then threw the other end out the window. Carefully, she stood on the table and lowered first one leg and then the other out the narrow square. Her hands trembled and her arms quaked with the fear and exertion as she lowered herself, hand over hand, down the rope.

She jumped the last three feet, landing hard on cobblestones slick with waste and discarded bits of refuse. Her hands felt raw, and when she looked at them, she saw that they were bleeding. However, there was no time to assess the damage. Althea forced her legs to walk, and then, when she was sure they would not give way beneath her, to run.

But to whom and to what, she could not be sure. Each turn produced nothing further than another fetid alley and more wretched persons half-dead from hunger or drink. Even in her present tattered state, Althea knew that the quality of her nightdress, if not the outward appearance of health, marked her for robbery or worse. Given the current sky, it must be late afternoon. It was only a matter of time before night would come with all of its horrors. No swiftness of foot would save her in the dark.

Already she could feel the eyes of the curious upon her. If only she could find some sign of where she was, she would know the direction in which to walk. Although, as she looked down at the remnants of her satin slippers, if it were more than a couple of miles, she would find herself barefoot on the cobblestones.

Then, in the distance, she caught sight of a church spire. A church! Of course, she could seek refuge there until some word could be sent back to Jane. She quickened her pace, moving in and out of the narrow lanes, always focused on the spire. She heard a murmuring commotion behind her and footsteps. She tried to move faster, but the fatigue of her escape made her legs feel torpid.

Around another bend, the church came into view ahead of her, no more than several hundred feet. She sped up. Just a few more steps and she would find refuge. But the voices were louder in her ears. They were calling out to each other. It was more distinct now—the shout of a mob about to attack. *I have become prey,* she thought, and she urged her feet forward. The church. She must reach the doorway. She felt the pull of hands on her arms, heard the rip of the fabric of her silk wrapper. Her head jerked back in pain as some unseen fingers pulled at her hair.

And then there was nothing.

CHAPTER TWENTY

Althea could hear voices through the wall. Men's voices raised in anger, but she didn't know why. Her head throbbed, and if she could have but moved her hands, she was sure they would have detected a large lump at the base of her skull, a product of whatever cudgel the mob had used to subdue her. She was fairly certain they'd taken her back to the location of her previous entrapment, but the darkness of the room and her current immobility made it impossible to know. She could feel the narrow bits of straw poke through the thin fabric of her nightdress and the telltale prick of insect pinschers upon her flesh, from which she deduced that someone had tied her to a poorly aired bed. Where were the spiders now when she needed them?

Surely Charles was at the root of her current predicament. He must have returned soon after her escape and sent the denizens of the neighborhood in search of her, likely with promises of money or drink. What a fool she had been to think that she could have escaped such a place. And yet her mind refused to bow to the inevitable. There must be a way, some mechanism to free herself.

At least he couldn't kill her until the vows had been exchanged. That was no little comfort. A trip to Gretna Green would require a carriage and time upon the road—time enough to devise another plan. In the interim, she might do well to make him think she had become resigned to her fate. He would assume that the beating had subdued her spirit.

Her thoughts ran unbidden to Jane. Jane wouldn't believe the story of the elopement, if indeed Charles had left word with his family, which Althea was beginning to doubt. Jane would know how unlikely Althea was to leave her house at night in such a manner. Perhaps Jane would attempt to find her. But what could Jane do, living at Levanwood House? What help could she possibly solicit? Bow Street? But would Jane even know how to reach Mr. Read? No, it was too much to hope. She thought of Norwich. He must have heard Pettigrew's lies. Perhaps his mind was not as attuned to hers as she had thought. If he listened to Pettigrew, he might believe her capable of any strange flight of fancy, even an ignominious elopement with another man.

The shouting in the next room ceased abruptly, and Althea heard footsteps and the sound of a creaky door swinging open. The pale light of a guttered candle showed the darkened silhouette of a man.

"Comfortable, my darling?" Charles said.

Althea didn't respond.

"You naughty child. You really shouldn't tease me by running away."

Charles set the candle on the table and then knelt down beside her. He reached over and smoothed the hair from her forehead. "How I love to see you thus, my sweet." She could hear the quiver of desire in his voice. "I think you and I shall play this game often when we are married."

"What game?" Althea's voice came out a hoarse whisper.

His hand stroked her forehead once more and then grabbed a hunk of hair and jerked her head back. Althea let out a cry of pain.

Charles laughed. "Why, release and catch Althea, release and catch." He stroked her forehead once more. "Come now, you shall grow to like it, I promise. And if you are a very good little girl, I might be inclined to treat you more kindly than the mob. Although, I cannot promise. There is something so lovely about watching you suffer." His voice dropped low. "More delightful than all the girls before."

"What girls?" she said, before she could stop her wayward tongue. Unfortunately, she already knew the answer. It was so simple, she should have tumbled to it long before.

He stood. "Jealous? You need not mind them."

"Was Mary one?"

"Eventually. But not on purpose, or at least, that wasn't my principal object." He paused. "There were others, of course. But servants are easy to come by in London, and I did enjoy it so very much."

"Even with your father's valet?"

Charles laughed softly. "No, that was different. He shouldn't have tried to make father pay for his silence. However, I did like the feel of the rope around his throat." Charles leaned down over her, his breath hot and sour on her cheek. "I had thought to give you the courtesy of waiting until our wedding night, but I find the excitement of your escape has made me desire to possess you sooner. In any case, as you are a widow, I shall have to get you with child to make the matter stick. You would like that, wouldn't you? Our own darling babe."

Althea heard the sound of rustling fabric, perhaps the fumbling of stiff fingers on small breeches buttons. Her breath caught in her throat. No. No matter what strategy she had to employ, she would never willingly submit. She thought of something her husband had once said to her as they examined the mottled frogs that made their home in the pond at Dettamoor Park. "All creatures are at their most vulnerable in the throes of the mating urges." This was true for the human as well as the frog. When Charles loosened the restraints on her legs, as he must given his diabolical purpose, she would have the strength to push him off, or at the very least kick him where he would feel most pain.

She had just decided to feign limp exhaustion until the crucial moment when she heard the sound of shouting coming from the floor below. Charles paused and stood upright, obviously listening to the ruckus underneath them.

Then, before Althea had time to even cry out, the door to the room burst open. "Where is she?" someone shouted. One of the figures held a lantern high, but it swung to and fro, throwing fearful shadows in every direction.

"He's going out the window!" shouted another. There was a scuffle as several pairs of feet rushed over to the ripped paper of the window. "He has a rope. Someone get down to the street and catch him!"

Two men dashed out the door. Althea could hear the thumps of their footsteps as they ran down the stairs. And off in the distance, the sound of a pistol shot. And then another. "Please, let them reach their intended target!" Althea prayed.

The man with the lantern swung it in her direction. "My God, she's over there," he said.

"What?" said a voice Althea knew well. How had Norwich come to find her?

"Yes, Lavender is right," replied a voice that sounded very much like Magistrate Read. "Come, Lavender, help me untie her. Lady Trent, are you hurt?"

But before she could reply, Norwich knelt down beside her and began to work the knots at her wrists. "I have no words, Althea, no words," he said.

At the sight of him Althea felt a rush of joy so powerful that she was momentarily bereft of speech. "How did you find me?" she finally got out.

Magistrate Read leaned over to work the knots at her feet. "Come Lavender, bring the lantern closer so we may be quick about our work. It was Miss Trent who first alerted us. She said that she had received some sort of letter saying that you had run off and knew that that could not be true. She contacted His Grace," Read nodded in Norwich's direction, "who had the fortunate thought to question some of the street urchins. One of them remembered seeing a man lifting a lady into a hack carriage early in the morning and remembered the carriage most particularly because it had a crest on the side that had been painted over."

"We were able to trace the carriage at least as far as this neighborhood," Norwich added. "Then it was just a question of asking the right people in the right sort of way. There, Lady Trent, can you move your arms?"

Althea stretched them up and winced. Her wrists felt as raw as her hands. "I don't think I have any broken bones, but my head does hurt fearfully."

"I will take you back to Norwich House, where my mother's own physician shall attend you. My sister is in residence now, so you need not worry about the proprieties," Norwich said.

"Thank you, but I can't leave dear Jane. We should make plans for our return to Dettamoor Park."

"In due time, Lady Trent," Mr. Read replied. "But first we must see to your injuries, and then you must tell us what you know about Lord Charles."

"Yes." Norwich undid the knot around her waist and pulled the rope free. "Here, let me help you. Can you sit up?"

Althea took his proffered hand. "I believe so." He pulled her up gently, but her head began to throb. She clutched his arm. "I feel so out of sorts, forgive me."

"Nonsense." In one swift move, he got his arms under her back and lifted her up, cradling her against his chest. Althea relaxed gratefully into his embrace, too exhausted to move. "Come Read, Lavender, Standon, hold the door for me, would you?"

CHAPTER TWENTY-ONE

It was several days before Althea felt well enough to leave her bed. But as soon as she was able, she sent a message around to Mr. Read. He arrived thereafter and was shown into one of the many formal sitting rooms in Norwich House. This one was called the yellow salon, but it failed by its ornate multicolored decoration to explain to its occupants how it achieved that name. Althea had been informed that Lady Bertlesmon favored another room, labeled the rose salon, but, as Althea had only made Lady Bertlesmon's acquaintance once since she had been so unexpectedly invited to stay, she could give no opinion on the relative merits of one or the other.

Mr. Read found Althea and Jane seated comfortably by a fire, Jane seemingly engrossed in her needlework and Althea seemingly engrossed in watching the flames in the grate. Jane set aside the handiwork and greeted him warmly. "Magistrate Read, how kind of you to pay us a visit. Lady Trent was quite anxious to discuss the matter of the Richmond Thief with you."

"It is very kind of you to come so quickly, Mr. Read. We have much to discuss." Althea smiled at him warmly. "And I have much to thank you for. Do please sit down." She indicated a space to her left on the settee.

Read sat down beside her. "It was nothing, madam. I am just glad that we reached your ladyship in time. Please tell me that your injuries are on the mend?"

Althea raised the sleeve of her gown to show a bandaged wrist. "Yes. Everything seems to be healing just as it ought. But let us talk of more important things. What is to be done with Charles's death? I fear there will be a great scandal. And you may speak freely in front of Jane, for I have taken her into my confidence in all important matters."

Read nodded. "No need to worry, Lady Trent. You perhaps have not seen the papers. Lord Charles was set upon by footpads. We are hard on the heels of the assassins, but I fear that they may never be apprehended."

"That is a good explanation. And Lord Bingham? Charles caused a carriage accident in order to kill his brother. And if that didn't work, he had paid someone to kill him as if during a robbery."

"That is still a bit of mystery. We found Lord Bingham's carriage smashed to bits, with the tiger wounded, but no sign of Bingham himself."

"No sign?" Jane said.

"None," Read replied. "We thought perhaps your ladyship might know what happened?"

"Charles assumed he was dead, but perhaps John was more intelligent. He's led a double life for so long, escape must be second nature."

"Double life?" Read said.

"He had a wife safely ensconced in a small house in a respectable, but not fashionable, neighborhood. She is a gentlewoman who lacks the dowry and noble parentage so necessary for the future Marquess of Levanwood. They met in Italy and secretly married abroad, but he feared to tell his family, especially since they needed him to marry position and money."

"How did your ladyship discover this?"

"John let drop that he had purchased a strand of pearls in Italy, which led me to believe that he had once been in love with a woman. And the tales of him did not add up, so to speak. People said he drank, but he never showed any sign of it. They said he stayed in bed until late in the morning, but Jane and I saw him returning to the house early in the morning, so we knew that his late rising had to do with his coming back from somewhere. Plus, he did not seem in a hurry to marry despite the fact that everyone could see that the financial affairs of the family required it."

Althea paused and then said, "And there was something about his continuous talk of poetry and his supposed fascination with morbid subjects. It was as if he wanted me to believe he was obsessed with poetry, and yet when we discussed other subjects, he would go for some time before mentioning it again. It struck me that he was playing a character on the stage, just as he played a wolf the night of the masquerade ball and played the debauched youth with his friends, drinking wine out of a skull-shaped cup. I decided to follow him, and that led me to his wife."

Read smiled. "Lord Bingham acted the part of a dissipated young man in order to hide his more conventional activities?"

"Yes. And his brother did the opposite—hid a life of evil behind a mask of respectability."

"How many persons had he harmed, do you think?"

"Too many," Jane replied with asperity.

Althea said, "Charles likely tried to kill more people than we will ever discover, but, aside from my own case and that of Lord Bingham, I know of at least two more. He killed his father's valet and the maidservant, Mary. But as I explained, that body in Hyde Park isn't her. She may be another victim of Charles, but I doubt it. He wouldn't have buried the body."

"How do you know this?" said Read.

"Let me start at the beginning of the story. The marquess took his own diamonds and claimed it was the Richmond Thief so that he could recover the money from Lloyd's and then sell the stones. One of his cronies, Lord Belfore, did the same several years ago. I became suspicious when I learned that he had enough money to hold the faro bank again. And Charles had admitted to me that the diamonds were insured."

"I'm sure I need not tell you that particular crime will be very difficult to prosecute. The marquess has some powerful friends who will try to prevent any hint of scandal from reaching him. I fear the shareholders of Lloyds will have to take it up if there is to be any justice in that quarter," Read said.

Althea nodded. "Unfortunately, you may be right. In any case, the marquess's valet found out and tried to blackmail the marquess. Charles learned of the plot and killed the valet by strangling him with a bellpull. Then he killed Mary when she saw the valet's body before it could be disposed of."

"But the maid wasn't Mary?" Read said.

"No. She'd been buried long before Mary went missing. I knew that because I found a larval specimen of *Dermestes trentatus*. As we discussed, my husband and I did a study of the beetle's life cycle. I took one home to compare with my notes, and it proved to me that the body couldn't be Mary because it would have had to be buried before Mary was killed. As you know, this method of detection will be presented in the forthcoming *Philosophical Transactions*."

"Perhaps you would be willing to prepare a simplified educational tool for my men to adopt? Definitive determination of when a body is disposed of would aid our work immeasurably."

"Of course. I also just found out that I have been invited to present my husband's manuscript on the subject in a fortnight, so perhaps you will wish to attend the lecture?"

"I would be delighted. But I digress. What happened to the bodies of the valet and Mary?" Read said.

"Resurrection men."

"Resurrection men?"

"Body snatchers for the medical trade—the unfortunate result of too few bodies available for anatomical studies for physicians. Charles studied medicine for a time and must have made connections. It was an easy way to eliminate the corpses of his victims and make some money on the side. I wish I had made the connection earlier. It would have saved me a painful experience."

Read shook his head. "So there is no Richmond Thief?"

"Perhaps there is, but not all of the thefts can be attributed to him. As I mentioned before, I think there are multiple causes. Many, including the Levanwood diamonds and the jewels of Lord Belfore, are the well-to-do trying to raise capital. I realized that when I examined your notes on each crime. Only a few seemed to be connected with the original theft of the Richmond earrings. Unfortunately, you will have the same difficulty bringing those culprits to justice as you do the Levanwoods, so I will leave it up to you as to how best to handle the high-society frauds."

"And what is your theory on the other crimes?"

"I would look at the registry offices to identify those persons who were hired for parties where the jewelry was stolen off the wearer. That can be attributed to a single thief or more likely a band of pickpockets masquerading as servants. Check particularly for cloakroom attendants. It has occurred to me that in the disorder of the women's cloakroom, clever thieves would find it quite easy to make off with any number of items without the wearer having the least notion. A lady would be distracted by putting her dress to rights, you see."

"A group of female thieves attempting to trade on the Richmond Thief's reputation?"

"Imitation is the sincerest form of flattery," Althea said.

Jane nodded. "I would be a good scheme if you think about it."

"And what about the crimes that do fit the pattern of the original Richmond theft?" Read said.

Althea hesitated, unsure of what she should say about Verlyn, when the door to the salon swung open.

"Your Grace." Read stood. "I was just consulting Lady Trent and Miss Trent regarding the Levanwood crimes."

"Mr. Read." Norwich nodded in his direction. "There cannot be too little said on that subject, but Lady Trent may not feel sufficiently strong to speak at length just yet."

Magistrate Read took the hint, saying, "Certainly. Lady Trent, Miss Trent, we shall discuss the matter further at another moment."

When he had been ushered out, Norwich addressed Jane. "I come bearing a message from my sister. She is feeling poorly this morning and asked most particularly after you as a companion for a quiet ride about town. She has some shopping to do, but doesn't quite feel up to the task. Perhaps you would be so kind?" The question hung in the air, and Jane, always alert to every scheme, jumped up and bustled out of the room without even a backward glance at Althea.

Norwich closed the door behind her. "I sent that fellow Pettigrew away. I told him that you were indisposed and in no mood for callers."

"Thank you," Althea said with relief. "I don't think I could stand an interview with him this morning."

"You are not actually engaged to Pettigrew, are you? I didn't want to think it, but many seem to take your engagement as unquestionable truth. His story of your previous interactions in Somerset was so very detailed."

"Of course not. It is all fabrication and misunderstanding. I wasn't paying attention to what he said to me when we danced at Lady Jersey's ball, and he took that as further agreement. At least that may be what happened. I don't rightly know. Believe me when I say that I have never knowingly agreed to be engaged to him. I am so very vexed!"

"Impudent puppy!" Norwich said with some heat, "I'll give him a set down the next time he comes, and we'll see if he dares to come by again."

"I know that I shouldn't be grateful, but thank you from the bottom of my heart. Even a day without Pettigrew is like a tonic for my nerves."

Norwich sat down beside her. "Then I shall be as rude as I know how to be."

"Your prodigious rudeness will surely keep him at bay for at least a week."

"I don't know if I should take that as praise of my general incivility or of Pettigrew's obtuseness."

"Both deserve to be recognized for their merits," Althea replied archly. "But let us not waste our time with Pettigrew, as I have been desiring private speech with you about another matter."

"Yes?" A half smile played across his mouth.

She took a deep breath. Norwich must be told about his brother's double life, even though Althea knew it was not the best way to repay all of his kindness to her. "We should discuss the Richmond Thief."

"Indeed, there is much I have to tell you." He took one of her hands gently in his. "Promise me that you will listen with an open heart."

"Open heart?" Althea looked down, unsure of what her hand in his could mean, but she did not remove it. She took another deep breath to steady her racing pulse. "Let us speak plainly. I have come to suspect that your brother, Lord George, is the true Richmond Thief."

She waited for the inevitable anger, but instead Norwich merely said, "I had guessed as much."

"About your brother?"

"No, about you. I knew that you would eventually come to that conclusion."

"So he's not the Richmond Thief?"

"He is, but it's not what you think. I'm sure you will keep what I am about to tell you in the strictest confidence. My brother has for many years worked to assist the government with clandestine diplomacy. It came to his attention that important information was leaking to the French government, and he sought to find out how."

"It was the jewelry, wasn't it? Starting with the Duchess of Richmond, I noticed that all of the thefts conforming to the Richmond Thief's methods had been recently refurbished at Howe and Cartwright's."

Norwich smiled. "I see I have not underestimated you. It was the boxes themselves, not the jewels. The Duchess and her compatriots were passing information to Bonaparte's government through a French jeweler employed by the firm. He in turn would pass instructions back in the boxes. George and the other agents had to steal the jewels to hide the true nature of the search. The jewels will be returned in due time when the operation is complete and the spy network destroyed beyond repair."

"So there was more than one Richmond Thief even with the thefts that conformed to the thief's pattern of crime?"

Norwich nodded. "No one person could have done everything the thief was purported to have done."

"But where is your brother now?" Althea said.

"Abroad on another mission. We don't expect him back for some time." Norwich regarded her with a strange expression, as if he were intent upon her reaction.

"I see. Well that is that. I must thank you again for—"

"No, Althea, it isn't. My brother wasn't the thief you knew." And then his voice dipped into a stage whisper that was all too familiar. "When George finally told me, I couldn't risk you finding out. Too much was at stake."

Althea's head had begun to spin. "And so you—"

"Yes. My God, Althea, you have no idea how I longed to tell you."

"I'm sure." She went numb with shock for a minute, and then anger surged within her. She pulled her hand away and cried out at the pain the movement caused the still-raw wound. She stood up, clutching her wrist, wanting to move, but feeling as if she might faint at any minute. "And you thought to treat me no better than—to kiss me—to make me believe that you loved me! I have never been so—"

"No!"

She looked up and realized that he was now pacing the floor in front of her.

"No, please do not say such things! I have been weak and deceitful, but it was only because I've been so out of my mind with love for you."

"With love for me?" Althea swayed, reached out and grabbed the arm of the settee for balance. "With love for me?"

"Yes, Althea. But knowing how you felt, knowing that I was the last man who could win your heart, I would have done anything to steal what couldn't be rightfully mine."

"I see."

He continued on, not seeming to notice the coldness of her remark. "Almost from our first meeting, I have come to feel for you a deep and abiding passion. And when I saw my chance to try to make you feel the same for me, I took it, damn the cost. But after everything that has happened, I find I cannot spend another day without confessing what I have done, because I want no secrets between us. I said that I would come to you as an honest man and beg your forgiveness. Well, here I am. Please forgive me."

"How is such a thing possible? You told me our courtship was just for show. You told me that you wished for our association to end. In short, you have done everything possible to show me how little we would suit as husband and wife."

Norwich stopped and held out his hand to her. "And you have done the same, but I cannot forget how you felt in my arms or how your sweet lips met mine. I almost lost you through my inaction and stupidity and will not contemplate the thought of parting from you now. Tell me that there is hope yet for me, Althea."

Althea regarded his hand with its large palm and strong fingers. She would be lying to herself if she didn't acknowledge the honor of the duke's proposal. It was more than she had ever allowed herself to imagine. "I don't know. This is all so strange. Why the deception?"

"I had to throw you, and Read for that matter, off the trail of the real situation. Despite my initial doubt, I had ample time to assess your abilities. I knew that sooner or later you would tumble to the truth, so I devised a plan to make you think that there was one Richmond Thief. And you helped me by wandering off to explore the darkened part of the house. Trust me when I say that I only intended to frighten you a little that first night in the library. However, my desire was greater than my virtue when I actually held you in my arms."

"Mine too, I suppose. Oh, I have been a fool!"

"I am the fool for hesitating when I heard Pettigrew's stories. I knew you disliked the man, but yet—I should have come to you then and confessed the whole at once. My delay was unpardonable, but please don't hide the truth from me now. Have I destroyed all my chances for happiness with you?"

"I don't know. I will not deny that I found pleasure in your embrace, but surely that cannot be the sole basis for—mutual regard and respect are essential for matrimony, are they not? Unless I have mistaken your intentions?"

Norwich laughed ruefully. "My intentions are the purest, although you may not believe it. Come Althea, say you will marry me."

She looked him in the eye. "Do you truly wish it?"

He returned her steady gaze with a look that seemed to melt the very bones of her body. "I have never wished for anything more in my life."

She thought of Arthur's proposal, based on reason and logic, so diametrically opposed to Norwich's impassioned speech. She had just gained her independence. Would she surrender it so easily? But the thought of those kisses made her feel that she had never truly understood what could be between a man and a woman. Her heart urged her forward, but her head held her back. There had to be a *via media*. "Yes, but on one condition."

He broke into a smile so radiant that Althea's heart began to flutter in her chest. *I am the moth*, she thought. She contemplated throwing her arms around his neck for a moment, but reason held her back. She was still too afraid of the flame.

"Anything," he replied.

"We shall keep the engagement a secret from all but the closest family for the next six months. If, at the end of that time, we haven't murdered each other, or you haven't grown tired of my independence and I of your domination, we can marry."

He started to speak, but she stopped him. "Before you agree, you must know that I intend to continue my scientific work, so you will have to keep your disgust of insects to yourself."

"Disgust?"

"One of the reasons I dressed as a beetle for the masquerade was to prove to you that they can be beautiful."

"You certainly proved that—to me and every gentleman there that night. I came to you as the thief even though I'd sworn never to do it again. You have no idea what the sight of you in that gown did to me. No, you can have no idea."

Althea smiled self-consciously. "Be that as it may, I will continue to study the real thing."

"I am prepared to endure any horror if it means I can have you. Do we have an agreement or not?"

"Yes." She placed her hand in his.

And before she knew what had happened, he pulled her to him and wrapped his arms tightly around her. "It will be a long six months." He leaned down and kissed her hard on the lips.

CHAPTER TWENTY-TWO

"I don't think I have ever been so nervous," Althea whispered to Jane as Jane accommodated herself beside Althea in the carriage.

"You will come through with your head held high as you always do."

"In any case, it is meant to be Arthur's work, so if I fail, it is of no matter."

Jane patted her hand. "There is always that."

Lady Bertlesmon climbed awkwardly into the carriage and landed with a thump on the opposite seat. "I don't know what my brother means by sending me along to this scientific meeting. Begging your pardon, Althea, this sort of thing is not my idea of an afternoon well spent."

"Stop your bellyaching, Minerva. A little knowledge would do you good," Norwich said as he settled in beside her.

Apparently, Norwich intended to be true to his word in support of Althea's scientific endeavors, although attendance at a speech was a far cry from mucking about in ponds and turning over the carcasses of dead things to get at the insects below, so time would tell. In any case, he had gone out of his way to be his best self during her sojourn at his house, only provoking one or two disagreements, and Althea had to admit that the idea of becoming his wife had become quite palatable to her. Quite palatable indeed.

Althea had expected Lady Bertlesmon to reject the secret fiancée so abruptly thrust upon her, but that lady seemed to take all of her brother's many whims in stride. Althea wondered if his mother would do the same when she returned from one of her long and frequent trips to Bath, but as her return was not imminent, Althea decided not to worry.

They soon found themselves at Somerset House, mingling with the throng of luminaries and attendant amateur scientists. Althea felt her pulse quicken with anxiety. She hoped Arthur would be proud of her. No, she mustn't think of him, or it would likely make her cry to think his dreams were now hers.

She felt a touch of her sleeve and looked up to see Norwich regarding her. "You shouldn't be nervous. Any woman who seems as familiar with corpses as you are cannot be nervous of a bunch of windbags, dabblers, and idle philosophers."

"Not nerves, I promise."

"You are a very bad liar, Althea. I shall remember that."

She smiled and then, turning her head, recognized a man standing off to her right. Mr. Read!

She caught his eye, and he hurried over. "Lady Trent, I have been anxiously awaiting your explanation of the use of insects in criminal detection."

"I shall hope that the Trent method is truly useful to Bow Street."

Read and Norwich exchanged greetings, and then Althea noticed another man beyond Read. My goodness, it appeared to be Cousin John. She tugged on Norwich's sleeve, and seeing where her eyes went, they quickly disengaged with Read, promising to discuss the Trent method at greater length after the presentation.

When they reached John, they could see that he was supported by a crutch on one side and a small dark-haired lady on the other.

"Lord and Lady Bingham," Althea said as she reached them. "How wonderful to see you alive and well!"

"And you, cousin. When I heard you were to speak today, I resolved to come and see if I could have a private word with you. If you would be so kind as to speak with me, that is." He looked up and, seeing Norwich, closed his mouth.

"Do not be alarmed, John. His Grace was one of the men who rescued me from your brother's clutches. As you can imagine, I did not go with Charles willingly."

"Much obliged to you," John addressed Norwich. "For my family, sir, I do not know that we can ever make amends."

Norwich replied, "You are not your brother's keeper. And in any event, I think you have suffered much at his hands."

Althea, recollecting her manners, turned to Norwich. "May I present to you Lady Bingham? I'm afraid she has lived quite retired of late, but I hope she will soon make her debut in society."

They exchanged pleasantries, and then Lady Bingham said, "It was a very close call, Lady Trent. When I received word of the accident, I flew to his side."

"Lizzie is a capital nurse, aren't you, my dear?" John said, and then turning to Althea, "Fortunately, I was smarter than Charles gave me credit for. I've known Charles was a bad egg for some time, at least with respect to me, but living as I was, I had to keep him from finding Lizzie at all costs. I saw the fight about my carriage as the ruse that it was and brought a pair of pistols and a trusted manservant along for the ride. When I took a turn and felt the carriage heave under me, I leaped free, breaking my leg but not my neck, and then rolled down the hill. My manservant jumped without injury and joined me at the bottom of the hill. We were able to find suitable cover behind a tree when some ruffians sought to finish us off."

He paused and met Althea's gaze directly. "I'm not sure what I thought would happen, but I did not expect Charles to stoop to murder, in my case or in yours. You must believe me that had I known, I would have done whatever I could to keep you out of harm's way."

"I do believe you," Althea said, "and it was marriage he wanted from me, not murder. Although, looking back upon it, death was certainly the preferable option."

John winced. "I can readily understand. My mother tells me that he was shot down by footpads."

Norwich looked John in the eye. "Yes, that is exactly how it happened."

John nodded in understanding. "After everything, I can't say that doesn't cause me relief. Although the proprieties were followed for the funeral. No need to bring society in to gawk."

"No," Althea replied, "that would not be prudent."

"Begging your pardon, we also thought it best to say that you accepted Lady Bertlesmon's most obliging offer to stay due to the mourning rigors at Levanwood House," John said.

"Oh dear," Althea said. "I shall have to observe mourning again, shan't I?"

"No more than two weeks, I think," Norwich said.

"I do hope that the financial situation is not as dire as Charles led me to believe," Althea said.

"Nothing that my father and I can't manage now that the truth is out in the open. Lizzie and I don't mind living in more retired circumstances, and my mother is frantic to leave London after everything that has happened. We shall sell the London house and pay Lloyds back as my father never got to the point of selling the necklace. He just told Charles that he had because he didn't want Charles to steal it out from under him. He understands that what he did was wrong, and he will make everything right with the Lloyds investors. Then we can decide if we need to sell the necklace for real to deal with any other outstanding debts."

Althea shook her head, not daring to ask if John was fully aware of the number of people Charles had murdered in the name of financial recovery, and certainly unwilling to burden him with the murders done in the name of pleasure. Instead she said, "I still cannot believe that such depravity was so well concealed behind such a proper facade."

John nodded. "True evil was not in the gothic stories you and I discussed, but rather in my own home. I don't think I have much heart for poetry anymore."

"Do not say that. I await your wolf man composition most eagerly. Instead of playacting, you should put your talents to good use."

John thanked her and would have said more, but the crowd began to fill the room.

"It is the moment of truth for me," Althea said.

They said their goodbyes, and Althea, extracting her prepared notes from her reticule, moved into position in the front of the meeting room. As she waited for the others to pontificate, she studied the plastered ceiling in all its glory, marveling at the twists of fate that had brought her there. It was with a jump that she heard her name and shook off her reverie.

"And today Lady Trent shall present a brief explanation of the use of *Dermestes trentatus* to determine the stage of forensic decomposition of animal matter. The Trent method of analysis, presented here today by Lady Trent, may be used in a number of circumstances, including the detection of the approximate time of death of persons discovered in the countryside, and should provide a great assistance to physicians called in for consultation in such matters. As all those present may remember, Sir Arthur Trent was a distinguished member of the Society, and at his untimely death he apparently had several monographs in preparation for presentation. Lady Trent has kindly agreed to compile these posthumous monographs for the benefit of the Society and to summarize Sir Arthur's work using the Trent method for us here today."

Althea stood and, pulling herself up to her full height, faced the great men of her generation. *Women do have the robust mental processes required for the hard labors of scientific investigation,* she told herself, *and one day they shall recognize me on my own!*

ACKNOWLEDGMENTS

I would like to thank my family, especially my mother, for helping me on my journey into Regency England. Dara, Cindy, and Kajal also deserve recognition for their editorial assistance. Thanks to my book group, viewers of Marshfield TV, and my other awesome fans in Marshfield, Saint Louis, and around the country. Thanks also to the libraries that have hosted my talks and supported my work. I hope my books continue to be checked out over and over. Also, thanks to Breanna and Brett for giving me opportunities to get the word out about all of my novels and to talk about books on *Writers and Readers of Central Wisconsin*. And finally, I want to thank my colleagues and friends at Security Health Plan for their continued support of my writing career.

ABOUT THE AUTHOR

Lisa Boero is a lawyer and moonlighting novelist. She is the author of the *Nerdy Girls* series of mysteries, featuring face-blind detective Liz Howe. Boero's third book, *Hell Made Easy*, is a dark comedy about lawyers in a battle of wits with the devil. *The Richmond Thief* is the product of the author's infatuation with Jane Austen and *Forensic Files*. It is her first historical mystery.

Lisa lives in Marshfield, Wisconsin, along with her family, and can be contacted at www.lisaboero.com.

Made in the USA
Middletown, DE
09 July 2018